'When I said  **didn't really**

'No?'

So Alex *had* heard. 'No,' Hannah sighed.

'It doesn't surprise me. You do and say a lot of things you don't mean!'

Colour flooded Hannah's cheeks. 'I guess it was because I was feeling so grateful.' At the look in Alex's eyes, she added quickly, 'Not because you were making love to me!'

'Of course not!' Alex answered drily.

Dear Reader

As spring moves into summer, you can't help but think about summer holidays, and to put you in the right frame of mind this month's selection is jam-packed with exotic holiday destinations. As a tempter, why not try Patricia Wilson's new Euromance, DARK SUNLIGHT, set in sultry Spain? *And*, who knows, you may well find yourself one day visiting the very places mentioned in the novel! One thing's for sure, you're bound to have lots of fun on the way...

The Editor

Rosemary Badger was born in Canada. At school she had a teacher who read to the class every day. Her reading was sheer magic. If the story was sad, the whole class sobbed. If it was funny, everyone roared. Rosemary had always loved reading but this teacher made her yearn to write! Rosemary now lives with her husband and four children in the beautiful town of Bundaberg, in Queensland, Australia, surrounded by glorious beaches and savouring the warm sub-tropical climate.

DANCING WITH SHADOWS

BY

ROSEMARY BADGER

MILLS & BOON LIMITED
ETON HOUSE   18-24 PARADISE ROAD
RICHMOND   SURREY   TW9 1SR

MELANIE,
This is for you!

First published in Great Britain 1993
by Mills & Boon Limited

© Rosemary Badger 1993

Australian copyright 1993
Philippine copyright 1993
This edition 1993

ISBN 0 263 78036 8

Set in Times Roman 11½ on 12 pt.
01-9306-42766 C

Made and printed in Great Britain

CHAPTER ONE

HANNAH BAKER noticed the red trail bike first. She could hardly miss it, parked as it was smack in the middle of her driveway. Next she saw the boy. He was kneeling in her front garden planting what certainly appeared to be two rose bushes. She parked her grey Volvo sedan beside the bike, got out and called to him.

'Hello there.'

Her voice had been pleasant enough and certainly loud enough for the boy to have heard, but apparently he hadn't, for he continued along with his task, slowly patting the earth around the bushes. Smiling, Hannah started to approach him, but something about the child's demeanour suddenly made her stop.

He looked so sad and lonely. His eyes weren't focused on the job but seemed to be staring straight ahead, peering at something only he could see. Abruptly he stiffened, suddenly aware of Hannah's presence. He shot to his feet and fixed her with a pair of startling blue eyes. His solemn face was handsome and he was deeply tanned. Straight black hair fell over his forehead and he was in need of a haircut. His clothes, blue jeans and a red sloppy jo, were grubby but expensive. But it was his eyes which arrested her attention. They seemed haunted!

'Who are you?' Hannah gently enquired.

The boy shrugged his shoulders. 'Just a delivery boy.'

Hannah smiled. 'Don't delivery boys have names?'

His eyes grew cold and wary. He had no intention of revealing his name. Hannah glanced at the rose bushes and said kindly, 'I'm afraid you've delivered those to the wrong address. I haven't ordered any roses.'

'They're compliments of Drummond's Garden Centre. Every household within a five-kilometre radius will be receiving them,' the boy informed her parrot-fashion. 'The grand opening's tomorrow. Hope you can make it.'

He rubbed the soil from his hands on to his jeans and headed towards the red trail bike. Mystified, Hannah started to follow him.

'Wait,' she said, and reached for his arm. 'Let me give you something for——'

With a sharp cry of protest the boy snatched his arm away. Hannah drew back in surprise. 'I wasn't going to hurt you,' she tried to reassure you. 'I only wanted . . .'

But the boy wasn't listening. He hopped on to his trail bike and started the motor. Hannah was certain she saw tears in his eyes. Totally bewildered, she watched him go and then turned to stare down at the two new rose bushes she had suddenly acquired. Mimi, her housekeeper, appeared at the lounge-room window. Hannah glanced up at her and Mimi shrugged her shoulders as if to say she hadn't known what to make of the boy neither.

'The lad knocked on the door and said he had two rose bushes to plant and asked where he should put them,' Mimi explained when Hannah joined her in the kitchen. 'Naturally I assumed you'd ordered them, so I said to put them with your other roses.'

'It's obviously some sort of publicity campaign,' Hannah mused thoughtfully as she pushed back her shoulder-length blonde bobbed hair from the sides of her face, hung the jacket of her tailored caramel-coloured suit on the back of a chair and loosened the bow at the neck of her creamy silk blouse. Her large beautiful eyes, more golden than hazel, were troubled as she added, 'I don't think I've ever seen an unhappier-looking child.'

'Work makes children unhappy nowadays,' Mimi chuckled as she removed a casserole from the oven.

Hannah sniffed appreciatively. 'Chicken?'

'And dumplings. I've set the table for you on the patio. There's a slight breeze and it's much cooler than in here.' Mimi smiled fondly at

Hannah. 'Now enjoy your meal, and don't fret about that boy.'

'I won't,' Hannah promised, and smiled into the kindly grey eyes of her housekeeper, set in the round cherubic face. Two days a week Mimi came to Hannah's lovely little sandstone cottage which lay nestled in the hills high above Queensland's Gold Coast, an hour's drive south of Brisbane on Australia's blue Pacific shores. The thriving, bustling Coast was where Hannah worked at her demanding profession as a solicitor, and she was always grateful to leave the heat and the crowds for the cool peacefulness of the mountains. Her favourite days were the two on which Mimi came and restored the cottage to its mint condition. An added bonus was Mimi's talent for cooking. There was always something delicious waiting for Hannah when she returned home from work.

After Mimi had departed for her own home, Hannah poured herself a glass of white wine and carried it out to the patio. Despite her promise to Mimi, she couldn't erase the image of the boy's face from her mind. He had worn the haunted, naked look of misery which usually stemmed from heartbreak.

The last of the evening sun splashed on to the edge of the garden bed, caught hold of something and shot out a dazzling beacon of light.

Curious, Hannah put her glass down on the table Mimi had set and went to investigate.

Half buried in the soft, dark soil surrounding the newly planted rose bushes was a glittering silvery object. Hannah picked it up... and froze. Lying across the palm of her hand was a very ugly-looking switch-blade knife! The blade was black and scarred, the extended silver blade dented and splotched with rust. She felt certain it belonged to the boy, and her heart filled with a cold dread. As a solicitor she knew only too well the perils awaiting not only the victims of such weapons but also their owners.

Drummond's Garden Centre, the boy had said. Hannah carefully removed a yellow tag from one of the bushes. The name, address and telephone number were printed on it. She suddenly realised she had heard the name many times before today. The address told her the Centre was located near by, but she couldn't place it. But then new businesses were springing up all the time on the Coast, and Drummond's Garden Centre was apparently one of them. With a thoughtful expression on her face, Hannah went into the kitchen and dialled the telephone number printed on the tag.

The phone rang several times before it was finally answered. When it was, the background noise was almost deafening.

'Speak up!' a strong male voice commanded as Hannah tried unsuccessfully to make herself heard above the din.

'Hannah Baker here,' she shouted into the mouthpiece. 'I'd appreciate some information about one of your delivery boys. He delivered——'

'Speak louder, please,' the crisp voice ordered, leaving her with no doubt that whomever she was speaking to was definitely the man in charge. 'I can barely hear you.'

'A boy delivered——'

'This is impossible.' The voice was edged with impatience. 'We open tomorrow. Ring then.'

Hannah heard the dialling tone and realised he had hung up. She frowned at his rudeness and replaced the receiver. Tomorrow morning she fully intended to be one of Drummond's first customers.

She awoke with a start. The alarm clock on her bedside table told her it was just past five o'clock. Not normally a light sleeper, especially on a Saturday when she liked to sleep in, she wondered what it was that had awakened her. She heard a noise and strained her ears in an effort to identify it. In a flash she remembered.

Remembered the sad, haunted blue eyes. The dangerous weapon. And the roar the trail bike's motor had made! So he had come back, then.

She'd rather thought he might. She swung her long legs over the side of the bed, grabbed her pale blue dressing-gown and slipped it on as she crossed to the window.

The boy had hidden the bike behind a clump of bushes and was stealthily making his way towards the garden. Hannah met him there just as he rounded the corner. He froze at the sight of her, his big blue eyes rounded in shock at such a surprise.

'Hello, delivery boy,' Hannah greeted him softly.

'I . . . I thought I'd drop by to see how your roses are doing,' he stammered, and his eyes darted swiftly to the ground and she knew what he was looking for.

'Nice of you to think about them so early in the morning,' she said, not unkindly. 'But you needn't have bothered—I checked them last night. As you can see, they're fine.'

The boy swallowed hard. 'You . . . you checked them last night?'

'Uh-huh,' she nodded. 'Soon after you left.'

His dark blue eyes narrowed suspiciously. 'You found it, then?'

'Yes,' Hannah answered quietly, 'I did.'

He held out his hand. 'May I have it back, please?'

She shook her head. 'I'm sorry, but I can't do that.'

'Why not? It's mine. You can't keep what doesn't rightfully belong to you.'

'Ordinarily that would be true,' she agreed, 'but not this time.' She sighed heavily. 'You sound like a clever guy—surely you must know switchblades are illegal weapons? I'm a solicitor,' she went on to explain. 'I've seen the damage they do and the trouble they cause their owners.' She watched him closely. 'Do your parents know you have such a weapon?'

The boy's face turned white, making his eyes appear almost black. He backed away from her. 'Keep my old knife,' he quivered. 'See . . . see if I care.'

He turned on his heel and raced down the driveway to where he had hidden his bike. Hannah's heart was heavy with despair as she watched him. She wondered what had troubled him the most—the fact that she was a solicitor or the mention of his parents? With an unhappy sigh she went in and dressed for her visit to Drummond's Garden Centre.

She found it easily enough, and, when she did, realised this was the place extensively advertised in the media. Reporters referred to it as a 'new age' tropical paradise while others claimed it to be a 'magical fairyland'. It had even been compared to Disneyland! But Hannah hadn't paid much attention. There was always something bigger and better popping up on the Gold Coast.

But now as she viewed the complex she had to admit that the reporters were right. It was a paradise and it was magical! There were sparkling blue ponds dotted with child-size paddle-boat steamers and miniature sail-boats. Some of the ponds had gaily coloured wooden bridges where children stood and tossed crumbs to majestic white and black swans accompanied by their offspring. Lush green pastures were sprinkled with frisky foals, soft-eyed calves and frolicking lambs. The little barns in their white corrals were painted with bright bold colours of yellow, green and blue. Hannah was absolutely enchanted. She watched children playing with the animals before finally joining the throngs of adults sweeping over what must be a hundred hectares of everything and anything one could possibly want for a garden. She wondered how on earth she would ever spot the boy or find the man who called himself Drummond.

And she knew there was such a man. Oh, yes! It had to be the very same man she had heard interviewed on her radio as she drove to work. His manner had irritated her. She honestly hadn't understood why reporters seemed to love him. He had sounded so smug...so arrogant...so smooth...so condescending. He was an engineer and hadn't hesitated to inform radio-land that he had designed and built everything at the Centre. Informing, my foot. Boasting was closer to the truth. Well, the advertising had certainly paid off. Tour buses were arriving one after the other, depositing even more people to add to the hundreds already there. Drummond would rake in a fortune.

There was a long queue fronting the largest building. The building was in the shape of a gigantic tepee, built with long, slender poles stained a light green. The tepee was open front and back and looked bright and airy.

'What's in there?' Hannah asked a young woman standing at the end of the queue.

'The main nursery,' the woman replied. 'I'm hoping to get a miniature orange tree to keep in my lounge-room.'

'An orange tree in your lounge-room?' Hannah repeated. 'Incredible!'

'Isn't it just? My friend bought an apple tree. It's so cute.'

Hannah tried to imagine an apple tree or an orange tree in her own lounge-room. Would the fruit wait patiently to be picked, or would it drop from the branches and roll across the carpet? 'Incredible,' she repeated.

'I hope they're not all sold out by the time I get through this queue,' the woman sighed. 'Everyone seems to be buying one.'

That's true, Hannah silently agreed. Miniature orange and apple trees were indeed popular, as many people had one or the other tucked under their arms. She decided to stay in the queue. It seemed the likeliest place to find Drummond. The complex must have cost a fortune to build, and he would want to be close to the money-making part of the operation. And once she found him, she would waste no time enquiring about the boy.

It was an hour before Hannah finally found herself in the nursery. An hour spent in the sub-tropical sun, squashed between hot bodies, jostled and pushed and shoved. But the nursery was surprisingly cool despite the number of people browsing between the many aisles, and she gave Drummond full credit for his engineering skills. The air was filled with sweetness from the dazzling array of produce lining rugged log shelves. She saw the miniature fruit trees and was glad to note that the young woman she had spoken to in the queue had managed to buy three. There was such a happy, carnival-like atmosphere that Hannah found herself about to accept a trolley from a fresh-faced youth decked out in a red and white striped uniform proudly bearing Drummond's name on the back of his smartly crisp shirt. Then she came to her senses and remembered she was here on business.

'I'm here to see Mr Drummond,' she told the youth, who looked more like a peppermint stick or a baseball player in his striped uniform than someone who worked in a garden centre. 'Is he in this building, do you think?'

'You might try the loading bay. I saw him there half an hour ago.' He lifted his arm and pointed. 'It's that way, at the back of the building.'

Hannah thanked him and deftly made her way through the crowds in the appointed direction. She was several feet from the loading bay when a deep, familiar-sounding voice brought her to an abrupt halt. Ahead stood a man like no man she had ever seen before! Something leaped in her chest and she realised it was her heart. It was Drummond. Had to be. Her breath caught in her throat and a not unpleasant warmth crept through her body. She realised she was staring, but was quite powerless to do otherwise.

Alex Drummond saw her approach from the shadows. The loading bay wasn't the place for the unwary. Trucks and fork-lifts roared in and out despatching and receiving produce. The area was restricted because it was dangerous. Either she hadn't noticed the 'Employees Only' sign or she had chosen to ignore it. Suddenly she stopped and stared straight at him. He felt mesmerised by her eyes. They were a strange golden colour, rimmed with black and flecked with green. Tiger's eyes! She was wearing a pink dress and her golden hair fell across her shoulders. Dappled sunlight drifted through the planned spaces between the logs and shrouded her in an ethereal glow. She looked mystical, wrapped in whispery shades of pink. A soft breeze crept between the logs and the fabric of her dress danced around her long, shapely legs. One of his employees spotted her and pointed to a large sign above her head.

'Can't you read, lady? This is a restricted area—employees only.'

'I want to speak with Mr Drummond,' he heard her say, and when she spoke her beautiful golden eyes were still locked to his. He moved up to her.

'I'm Alex Drummond.'

Hannah gazed helplessly up at the darkly handsome man towering above her and was confronted with a pair of brilliant blue eyes set in a ruggedly handsome face. His mouth was full and chiselled, the jaw wide and strong. He was deeply tanned with laugh-lines around his eyes. A cleft darkened his chin and male dimples stroked his hard cheeks. A black pullover stretched across his broad shoulders and faded blue jeans hugged the muscular contours of his thighs. His hair was raven-black, thick and unruly. He was undoubtedly the most handsome man Hannah had ever seen. He was also the most virile. His masculinity fairly oozed from his very pores, and she felt its potency.

'I . . . I'm Hannah Baker,' she breathlessly returned the introduction.

His eyes, the mysterious colour of a deep blue ocean, drifted slowly over her, taking in every detail—the sun-bleached strands of hair streaking through the glistening gold. His hand moved as if to touch it. Long, silky lashes framed the strange beauty of her eyes and cast small shadows across the curves of her cheeks. Her complexion was creamy smooth and tinged with a warm pink. He knew it would feel like satin against his hands. Her lips were parted, strawberry-moist, and his own mouth hardened. He felt a stirring warmth in his groin. Hannah's heart pounded in her chest and blasted in her ears. She could scarcely breathe. Her breath stopped altogether when his eyes lingered on the enticing swell of her breasts. Mercifully, his eyes continued their seductive journey and travelled over the small waist, the practically non-existent hips and down the shapely calves to the dainty ankles and feet encased in white sandals. He took a deep breath and let it out slowly as though he had indeed taken a long journey, and finally settled the deep blue of his eyes on to the tawny goldness of hers. The seductive journey hadn't offended her. She felt exhilarated!

'What did you wish to speak to me about?' he asked, and his deeply sensuous voice sent another rippling wave of awareness throughout her body. This most definitely wasn't the arrogant, patronising voice she had heard over her car radio, but it was every bit as smooth.

Hannah cleared her throat and tried to regain her usual composure. 'Yesterday, a young boy delivered two rose bushes to my home,' she began.

Drummond nodded and smiled. 'A goodwill gesture for my neighbours.' She had obviously come to thank him.

'I was hoping you might provide me with some information about that boy.'

He frowned. 'What sort of information?'

'His name and address.'

'May I ask why?'

'I . . . I'd like to thank him. You see, not only did he deliver the roses but he also planted them.'

'It was all part of the job. The boys were well paid for their efforts.' His smile was warm on her face. 'I'm glad you were pleased.'

'I . . . I was.' For a moment she lost herself in that smile. Extracting information from this man wasn't proving easy. She decided on another tactic.

'While he was planting the roses, he . . . he lost something—it must have fallen from one of his pockets. If you could tell me where he lives, I could return it.'

Alex chuckled. 'Boys are forever losing something or another.' He held out a tanned hand with long, tapered fingers. 'Give it to me and I'll put it on our display board. He'll see it and claim it.'

Hannah's cheeks paled. The last thing the boy needed was for his switch-blade to be put on display. It would almost certainly cost him his job, and, for all she knew, his family might be dependent on his small wage, although he had been well dressed. She shook her head.

'I'd like to return it to him personally.'

His eyes narrowed shrewdly on her face. 'I take it we're not discussing trivia here?' he asked quietly.

'No,' she sighed, 'we're not.'

'And you obviously have no intention of telling me what it is the boy lost,' he concluded correctly.

'No—I'm sorry.'

Alex studied her thoughtfully for a few seconds, liking her quiet determination. 'All right,' he agreed. 'Perhaps if you describe him I might be able to help you, although I'm not familiar with all the boys. Most of the younger ones were only hired for the deliveries.'

Hannah had no doubt this particular boy wouldn't be forgotten. She smiled gratefully up at Drummond and once again was struck and affected by his boldly handsome features. Then, quite unexpectedly, she experienced a feeling of uneasiness. It was strange how the boy's features were so like the man's...

'He...he's about this tall...' and she made small jabbing gestures with her hand until she thought the height was correct. 'He's got dark hair and...blue eyes. I think he might be thirteen or fourteen.'

Alex Drummond started to look impatient. 'You'll need to be more specific. That description fits any one of a number of lads.'

'He had a red trail bike.' She tore her eyes from his and stared miserably down at her white sandals.

'A red trail bike?' he repeated, and she felt rather than saw sudden tenseness of every muscle in his body. 'Are you certain?'

She nodded and her misery grew. 'Yes.'

'Why are you so determined to find this boy?' His voice had lost its warmth.

Hannah raised her eyes to meet his. 'Because I believe he might be in trouble.' She added with a sigh, 'Either that or headed straight towards it.'

'What sort of trouble?' He grabbed her arm. 'What did you find?'

'That's only for his parents to know.'

Exasperation flared in Drummond's eyes. 'I'm his uncle!'

She wasn't in the least surprised. There was such a strong family resemblance that she had thought he might be the boy's father. 'I'm sorry,' she said, 'but an uncle isn't the same as a father. I'd very much like to speak with his parents.' She added gently, 'I'm a solicitor, you see, and I've done a lot of work with children. Sometimes a little talk from someone like myself helps . . .'

Drummond tightened the grip on her arm. He glanced quickly towards the loading bay and said in a low voice, 'If my nephew's in trouble I want to hear about it.' His eyes seared hers. '*Now*!'

'Let go of my arm,' Hannah gasped as she struggled to loosen the vicelike grip.

He slipped his hand down to her elbow and propelled her towards a door, thrust it open and steered her none too gently inside. It was an office, small and cluttered, with a huge desk, a computer, filing cabinets and a long, low table covered with containers of soil samples and small seedlings. A large window looked out on to the garden complex. Hannah viewed all this in a twinkling before she heard the door slam behind them and the feel of strong hands on her shoulders as she was spun around to face the storm in Alex Drummond's eyes.

'What do you have that belongs to my nephew?' he demanded harshly.

'His parents——'

'Are dead!'

The words hit her like blows. 'Dead?' she repeated hollowly.

He nodded, his expression grim. 'Over a year now. They were killed in a light plane crash.' He spoke brusquely, obviously not wanting to dwell on the tragedy. 'Bartholomew is the eldest—

thirteen. He has two younger sisters, Josephine, twelve and Annabelle, eight. They live here with me.'

Hannah struggled to take this in. The boy with the haunted blue eyes was an orphan. He had two sisters, Josephine and Annabelle. She liked the sound of their names. They were old-fashioned, unusual. She was aware of Alex Drummond's dark brooding eyes watching her, and a cold knot formed in her stomach. How could she tell him what she had found? How could she *not* tell him? She took a deep, steadying breath and let it out slowly.

'I have his switch-blade knife.'

A stunned silence followed her announcement, broken finally by a short, sharp burst of disbelieving laughter. 'Bartholomew with a switch-blade? Don't be ridiculous!'

CHAPTER TWO

'I'M SORRY, but it's true,' Hannah stated quietly.

Alex's eyes hardened as he looked at her and an angry flush stole across his hard cheeks. He couldn't believe the nerve of the woman, barging in here with her wild accusation. She watched him with those strangely beautiful eyes and didn't even have the decency to shrink a little under his harshly penetrating glare.

'You said this . . . this object dropped from my nephew's pocket while he was planting, free of charge, the two rose bushes which you received, also free of charge, in your garden. Is that correct, Miss Baker?'

If the situation hadn't been so grave Hannah might have been amused that Alex Drummond was interrogating her. She had done just this sort of thing many times in the courtroom, but this was the first time she had ever found herself in the witness box. 'That's correct, Mr Drummond.'

'And of course you actually saw this object fall from my nephew's pocket?'

'No, actually, I didn't.'

Alex's eyes widened in mock surprise. 'You didn't see it fall from his pocket, but you claim it to be his?'

He's really very good, Hannah thought, annoyed. If this had been a real court she could imagine the snickerings his line of questioning would have provoked. She sat straighter in her chair.

'Well, Miss Baker,' he continued in that same maddening drawl, 'when *did* you see the knife?'

'Later.' She cleared her throat. 'I was sitting on my patio when I saw a flash of light. I got up, curious as to what it might be. That's when I saw it.'

'By "it" you mean the knife?'

An angry flush swept across her cheeks. 'Yes,' she answered tersely.

'And was that *after* my nephew had left your property?'

'Yes, it was.'

'So you just assumed the knife was his.'

'I *knew* it was his.'

'How so?'

'Because it wasn't there before!' Hannah snapped.

'Because it wasn't there before,' he repeated mockingly. He bent down, placed his hands on either side of her chair and warned in a chilling voice, 'I don't take kindly to people falsely ac-

cusing members of my family.' A hand shot out
and cupped her chin. 'Do I make myself clear?'

He was angry and so was she, but that did
nothing to quell the tingling sensation she felt at
his proximity. She felt herself drifting into the
cobalt-blue of his eyes and her sensitive skin
burned beneath his fingertips. He pushed himself
away from the chair and stood gazing down at
her. She saw the contempt in his eyes.

'I haven't come here to accuse anyone,'
Hannah said in a tremulous voice. 'All I wanted
to do was to try and help a young boy who...who
looked so sad.'

For a brief instant she thought she saw a look
of anguish pass over Alex's eyes. Despair seemed
to wash over his rugged features. He lifted a hand
and rubbed it roughly across his jaw as if to scrub
it away. Hannah felt a gnawing ache in her heart.

'Bartholomew returned to my house this
morning,' she continued quietly. 'He came to
look for the knife. When I refused to give it to
him he...he became very upset and ran away.'

Alex stood motionless as he listened and his
expression was tight and grim. 'Where's the knife
now?' he asked curtly.

'Here...in my bag.' She opened the zip of her
white leather shoulder-bag and removed a
package wrapped in brown paper. She handed it
to him and he placed it on his desk, unwrapped
it and stood staring down at the ugly object, his

hands thrust deeply into his pockets, his back ramrod-stiff. He pressed a buzzer. 'Mac, page Bartholomew for me,' he ordered curtly. 'Tell him to come to my office immediately.'

'Sure, boss.'

They could hear the repeated command of the request drifting through the opened window, while Alex impatiently tapped his fingers on the desk top. He stabbed the buzzer again. 'Never mind, Mac. It's lunchtime. He must be up at the house.'

Hannah felt an enormous sense of relief sweep through her. She had alerted Alex Drummond to the possible dangers awaiting his nephew. He was a sensitive, intelligent man who obviously cared deeply for the boy. He would know what to do. Hannah stood up and thrust the strap of her bag across her shoulder. Alex wrapped up the knife, tucked the bundle under his arm and grabbed a set of keys from the desk. Hannah searched her mind for something appropriate to say.

'Good luck,' she managed. 'With Bartholomew and your new business.'

He grabbed her arm. 'You're coming with me!'

He led her outside to a sturdy-looking Range Rover parked behind the loading bay. He helped her into the vehicle and slammed the door shut. Ice had settled over his eyes and she knew he was seething inside. He slid behind the steering-wheel and tossed the brown paper parcel on to the space

separating them. Hannah stole a glance at his
profile and shivered. He looked as if he had been
carved from stone. The vehicle shot forward and
she turned her attention to a more pleasant view.

Orchards, their boughs laden with tropical
fruits, lined either side of the dirt road. The air
was heavy with their sweetly exotic scents.
Workers toiled between the neat rows and small
tractors, driven by bare-chested men, their tanned
backs gleaming with sweat under the hot sun,
zipped in and out around the trees, loosening the
rich red soil. The men waved cheerfully as the
Rover roared past them.

The orchards gradually gave way to a clearing
where several hectares had been prepared for
small crops. The soil looked rich and fertile.
Healthy dark green plants grew in straight rows
while irrigation sprinklers spun crazily above
them. Hannah wondered what it would be like
to run barefooted in that thick, soft, warm-
looking soil.

'Are those strawberries?' she asked, hoping for
conversation.

'They are.' Alex's voice was clipped.

'I love strawberries.' She hoped he wouldn't
think she was hinting for some, and when the
seconds ticked by without him offering to give
her any she realised with chagrin that if she
wanted any she would have to buy them. Alex
Drummond had no intention of becoming

friendly or neighbourly. Well, that was fine with her. She would buy her strawberries from the supermarket, certainly not from him!

The Rover climbed a small hill and over the rise a majestic white colonial mansion came into view. It was double-storeyed with delicate white wrought-iron lacework enclosing the wide sweeping verandas, top and bottom. Tall, stately french windows opened on to the verandas while brilliant scarlet bougainvillaeas tumbled their tropical blooms in a wildly glorious abandonment up and around the sides of this impressively beautiful home.

On the steps leading up to the veranda sat a boy and a girl. Hannah immediately recognised the boy. On seeing the Rover and the young woman occupying the passenger's seat, Bartholomew sprang to his feet and darted up the stairs. The girl started to follow, and Hannah guessed correctly that this was his sister Josephine. Bartholomew shouted something to her and she stopped, uncertain as to what she should do. She stood nervously on the step and watched Bartholomew race into the house, then she turned to see her uncle striding purposefully towards her. Hannah reluctantly followed. She felt, suddenly, like the wicked witch.

'Josephine, this is Miss Baker,' Alex briskly introduced his niece to Hannah. 'Where did your brother fly off to in such a hurry?'

'I...I don't know,' she answered hesitantly. Her eyes were the same deep blue as her uncle's and brother's.

'Take Miss Baker into the lounge-room,' Alex instructed her, 'while I see to your brother,' he added grimly, and bounded up the stairs two at a time and passed through the same door Bartholomew had only moments earlier. Hannah and the child listened to the sound of his footsteps thundering down the long wooden hall.

'You...you're not going to make trouble for Bartholomew, are you?' Josephine asked Hannah anxiously, and pushed her long, straight black hair away from her face. She was tall like her brother but thin rather than slender. Dressed in a faded blue dress and with her pale skin and violet-coloured eyes, she gave the impression of being a child from a previous century. Hannah's heart went out to her. She looked so lost...so alone.

'Of course not,' Hannah answered gently, and added reassuringly, 'I only want to help him.'

Josephine wasn't at all convinced. 'That's not what my brother told me.' She hesitated. 'He said you were going to tell lies about him to Uncle Alex.' Her grave little voice trembled and she looked pleadingly up at Hannah. 'Please don't,' she added in a whisper. 'Everything's just starting to get nice. Please don't spoil it.'

There was such desperation in the childish plea that Hannah was at a loss as to what to say. 'I promise not to tell any lies,' she finally managed, and as she spoke there was the sound of a trail bike coming from somewhere at the back of the house. The motor was abruptly cut and they could hear Bartholomew's loud angry shouts of protest. With a sinking heart Hannah realised the boy must have tried to escape and Alex had stopped him. Beside her, she felt Josephine tremble.

'Uncle Alex said I was to take you into the lounge-room.' Josephine looked hopefully up at Hannah. 'Unless you'd rather go home? I could tell him . . .'

She broke off when Hannah laid a gentle hand on her thin little shoulder. 'No, I think we'd better do what your uncle suggested.'

There was the strong smell of fresh paint and plaster as Josephine led Hannah down the long wide entrance hall to the lounge-room. The floorboards had been sanded, exposing the beauty of rich, honey-coloured pine. Halfway down the massive hall was a grand staircase sweeping up to the second floor. Josephine opened a door and politely stood aside for Hannah to enter.

'This is the lounge-room,' she explained. 'You may wait in here.'

'Thank you,' Hannah smiled. 'Are you going to wait with me?'

But Josephine wasn't listening—at least, not to Hannah. Her dark head was slightly tilted. Echoing down the hall were the voices of her uncle and brother. Bartholomew's was argumentative, Alex's deeply patient. Josephine shut the door, leaving Hannah on her own. She could hear the child's footsteps hurrying towards the sound of the voices. Hannah shook her head and sighed. Josephine was on her way to act as peacemaker, this she knew.

The lounge-room was huge, the walls broken by the french windows opening on to the veranda. There was an impressive marble fireplace, the grate empty. The odour of fresh paint wasn't as strong here, but the eye could see that the walls had been newly coated with a soft grey. An old carpet had been ripped from the floor, rolled into a cylinder and lay across the naked boards. A handsome brown leather suite was pushed into a corner and partially covered by a sheet splattered with droplets of grey. From one of the french windows was a view of a swimming-pool. A man dressed in white overalls was laying tiles around its exterior. The pool was obviously new and as yet hadn't been filled with water. Renovating a homestead the size of this one would cost a fortune, Hannah knew from even the small changes she had made at her little cottage. She looked again at the pool. Obviously Alex Drummond wanted only the best for his three charges. She wondered anxiously how his discussion with Bartholomew was going. And why had he insisted she come to the house if she wasn't to be a part of it?

Suddenly she got the distinct impression that she wasn't the only one in the room. She turned abruptly. Standing just inside the door was a small girl. Violet-blue eyes seemed to take up the whole of her little face. Her black hair had been brushed and teased into a frizzy halo and her lips were painted a bright orange. She wore a shimmering gold gown dotted with sequins, the bodice baggy, the full skirt held out at the sides by dainty hands, the nails painted a shocking purple. Hooped earrings dangled from her tiny lobes while strings of beads and chains circled her delicate neck. Her small feet were tucked into a pair of black, dangerous-looking stiletto slingbacks.

'Good afternoon, Miss Baker,' the child drawled in a low, husky voice. 'My name is Annabelle Drummond.'

Hannah grinned. 'Good afternoon to you, Miss Drummond.'

Annabelle curtsied, and Hannah's grin widened. 'That's very good. Who are you supposed to be?'

The child wobbled across the room, a miniature Greta Garbo. She stopped at the fireplace and struck a dramatic pose. All she needs, Hannah thought, greatly amused, is a long gold cigarette holder to complete the picture. She chuckled and went over to Annabelle, where she was treated to a full view of the child's make-up.

Pencilled-in brows arched dramatically over the beautiful blue eyes framed with sweeping false lashes. A variety of perfumes, oils and colognes fought for supremacy and were responsible for Hannah taking a quick step backwards... and then another.

'Is that your costume for a school play?' Hannah asked admiringly while marvelling at the artistry of the make-up.

'Costume?' the child sniffed disdainfully. 'This...' and she glanced proudly down at her gown '...isn't a costume. This is just a dress.' She added grandly, 'An everyday dress.'

'I should see you when you get dressed up, huh?' Hannah chuckled. 'And what about that make-up? Is that for everyday as well?'

'Of course.' Annabelle picked up her skirts and swept over to one of the huge leather armchairs. Hannah watched, fascinated, as she flicked off the cover sheet and settled herself into it. She arranged her skirts, straightened the bodice and crossed her legs before peering at Hannah beneath long, fluttering lashes.

'Well, now,' she drawled in that peculiar husky voice, 'what's this I've been hearing about you?'

The corners of Hannah's mouth twitched, but she dared not smile. Annabelle Drummond was holding court!

'What have you heard?' Hannah enquired, her tone serious.

'That you're hellbent on causing trouble for my brother Bartholomew!'

'Watch your language, Annabelle,' a deep voice warned from the doorway.

Annabelle jumped up from the chair. 'Sorry, Uncle Alex. It just sorta slipped out.'

'Apologise to Miss Baker.'

'Sorry, Miss Baker.' There wasn't a shred of sincerity in the young voice.

'Apology accepted.' Hannah's eyes sparkled with amusement.

Alex frowned at his niece. 'What's that on your face?'

'Make-up.' She smiled hopefully up at him. 'Do you like it?'

'Not at all. Wash it off immediately.'

Annabelle's face crumpled and she began to cry. 'Miss Baker liked it,' she sniffed, and rubbed her balled little fists into her eyes. The results were immediate and disastrous. After she had flounced, deflated, from the room, Alex turned to Hannah.

'You *liked* it?' he asked with a shudder.

Hannah gave way to her laughter. 'Little girls love to experiment. I thought she was absolutely adorable.'

But Alex was far from amused. 'When you've stopped giggling, perhaps you wouldn't mind sitting down so we can discuss the other source of your amusement.'

The laughter died on her lips. 'What other source of amusement are you talking about? And I wasn't *giggling*, I was——'

'Tittering, then.' He indicated the chair Annabelle had vacated. 'Sit.'

Hannah's cheeks burst into flames. How dared he speak to her as if she were one of his charges? She was about to protest but the hard look in his eyes made her think better of it. She settled for a glare which didn't seem to faze him in the least and sat stiffly down in the chair. Alex remained by the fireplace, arm stretched along the mantel, the dark censure deepening in his eyes as he watched her.

'You arrived out of the blue,' he began in a low harsh voice, 'turned my household upside down with your wild accusations and insinuations, and, as if that wasn't enough, you've seriously interrupted the launching of my new business.'

'I...I'm sorry,' Hannah whispered. She raised her hands and dropped them helplessly. 'I didn't mean——'

'Silence!' he snarled. He crossed the room and pulled her to her feet. 'What are you *really* after?'

She shook her head. 'I...I don't know what you mean.'

'I mean *this*!' His eyes seemed to burn into hers before he pulled her against him and she felt the jolt of his hard thighs against the softness of her own, her breasts pressing against the muscular wall of his chest, his ragged, uneven breath fanning her cheek before the shocking thrill of his hard lips claiming the yielding softness of her own. The kiss was punishing and angry, but Hannah clung to him, kissing him back with a fierceness that matched his own. It was as if they had been caught in a violent storm, buffeted by the gales of a savage harmony which neither wanted rescuing from. As suddenly as it started, the storm abated. Alex abruptly set her away from him, his hands clamped to her shoulders. The silky strands of her golden hair fell against the roughened backs of his hands. His glittering eyes left the smoky passion of her own and he looked at the golden threads for several long seconds before he released her and Hannah felt herself sinking into the chair as if she no longer had a will of her own.

There was a knock at the door, and Alex ran his hand swiftly through his hair. It was dreadfully mussed. Hannah's cheeks burned with shame. She knew she was responsible. Alex opened the door with the unsettling calmness of one who had just been reading a newspaper and accepted a tray from a middle-aged, grey-haired woman who Hannah assumed correctly was the housekeeper.

'Thank you, Mrs Buckley,' he said. 'I'll bring the tray out to the kitchen when we've finished.'

'*We've*'! Hannah thought. So she was expected to dine with the man. Her hand fluttered up to her mouth. Her lips were still burning from his kiss. She watched Alex cross the room and place the tray on a low table. He grabbed two large cushions and dropped them on the floor in front of the table, then turned to her. She was sitting stiffly in the chair, pink staining her smooth cheeks, a wild look in her tiger eyes.

'Come and eat,' he ordered with a growl.

Hannah shook her head. 'I . . . I can't.'

'Why not?'

'I . . . I'm not hungry.'

'You must be.' He added mysteriously, 'After all the hard work you've done!'

She drew her fine tawny brows into a puzzled frown before once more shaking her head. 'I rarely eat lunch.'

'Then let this be one of the rare occasions when you do.'

It would seem churlish to continue to refuse. Hannah rose slowly and reluctantly made her way to the table. Alex indicated one of the cushions.

Both were covered in a thick green velvet. 'You can sit on that. I think you'll find it quite comfortable.'

So she was expected to sit on the floor. It didn't matter. What did concern her, though, was how she was going to sit in such close proximity to a man who had kissed her as she had never been kissed before, with such a wildly fierce passion. And she had returned that kiss in exactly the same manner. The colour in her cheeks deepened with renewed shame. She sat stiffly down on the cushion and carefully avoided any contact with those deep blue eyes which were partially responsible, she knew, for the strange hold he wielded over her.

She would eat a bit of lunch and listen to his account of his discussion with Bartholomew, for surely that was the object of his inviting her to share his meal. Later, when she was safely installed in her own dear little cottage, she would try to analyse what had happened here and then, with luck, forget it. The thought cheered her somewhat, but not as much as she would have wished.

Sitting next to him like this, each on a cushion in front of a small, low table, wasn't a good start. His hard shoulder was firmly pressed against her own, and while she managed to avoid his eyes she couldn't help noticing the silky black hairs curling so beautifully against the deep tan of his forearms.

The lunch was simple and unimaginative, certainly not to be compared with the tasty dishes Mimi whipped up for her. Hannah nibbled on a ham and tomato sandwich and wondered if Alex would have preferred something hot and far more nourishing for his lunch. After all, he was a busy man and probably starving by the time lunch rolled around. Not that she really cared, of course. In fact she was deeply grateful that the meal was so simple, because it meant it wouldn't take long to eat and soon she would be free to go.

'I had a talk with Bartholomew,' Alex began casually as he poured and handed Hannah a glass of fruit juice. 'It seems you were badly mistaken.' His eyes were cold on her face. 'He found the knife in your garden while he was digging a hole for the rose bushes. It was old and rusty and he figured it didn't belong to anyone, so he put it in his pocket. When he got home and saw he no longer had it, he decided to go back and look for it.'

Hannah frowned. 'But if that's true, why did he run off? Why didn't he simply tell me he'd found it?'

Alex took a long drink from his glass and then placed the empty vessel down on the table with a sharp bang.

'Perhaps he would have...if you hadn't threatened him!'

'Threatened him?' she repeated, eyes rounded in astonishment. 'I didn't——'

'You refused to give him the knife and told him you're a solicitor. He's a child, for goodness' sake. He thought you were going to take him to court, put him in gaol.'

'I'm sorry, I didn't mean——'

Alex sprang to his feet with surprising ease and agility for such a big man. He pulled her up with him and, with his hands on her slender shoulders, delivered the final blow.

'I'm quite used to women going to extraordinary lengths to introduce themselves and try to gain my favour. Usually I'm amused and sometimes flattered. But not this time.' His fingers dug into the fragile bones of her shoulders and his eyes were like chips of ice. 'You've laid blame and accusation at the feet of an innocent child. You've upset his sisters and worried the hell out of me!' The caustic tone of his voice was only surpassed by the bitter censure of his eyes. 'You pretended to be a so-called do-gooder,' he continued scathingly, 'and because your devious little ploy was original you almost had me fooled. *Almost*!'

Hannah stared up at him, her face drained of colour. Stunned by the accusation, she was shocked into silence. Alex mistook this as confirmation of her guilt, and the contempt in his eyes soared to new heights. His hands dropped from her shoulders.

'I want you to leave my house,' he stated frostily, 'and never set foot on my property again!'

CHAPTER THREE

THERE was a sharp tap on Hannah's office door.
'Come in,' she answered, and put the apple she
had been about to eat for lunch back on to her
desk. Mike Thompson, colleague and friend,
burst into the room. He was excited, agitated, his
fair skin flushed and his blond hair unruly. His
suit, as always, looked in need of a press.

'Hannah, you've got to help me! I've just received word that my people want to settle out of
court. Tyson's—you know the case.'

Hannah nodded. Mike had been working on
a compensation case for the past year, a case
which had left him feeling frustrated on more
than one occasion. He had done his best to convince his client that settlement outside of court
was their only hope. Now, apparently, Mike's
client had finally come to his senses.

'That's wonderful news, Mike,' she congrat-
ulated him. 'But I'm not up on all the details.
How can I help?'

'I don't need help with the case. It's another
client I'm concerned about. He's due in twenty
minutes. It's too late to ring and set another appointment. Besides, I wouldn't want to risk it.

43

He's big! He's important! He's *money*! He's also
very busy, and he wouldn't take kindly to a can-
cellation.' Mike glanced quickly at his watch.
'And I've got to get going. Will you handle him
for me?'

It would mean her lunch break, but Hannah
didn't mind. Mike had stood in for her more than
once when the unavoidable had happened. 'Of
course I will,' she agreed willingly. She glanced
at the files he was carrying. 'Is everything in
there?'

'Yup.' He handed them to her. 'It shouldn't
take long. Trust funds have been set up, and we
need signatures on all the pages and a cheque.
He's important, as I've said. Give him plenty of
those Hannah Baker smiles,' he added teasingly.
'And coffee . . . the perked stuff, not the instant.
And if he invites you to lunch, go! This guy's
got lots of money to invest. He's just sold his
aeronautical engineering plant in Sydney and
plans to build another one here. His latest project
on the Coast has attracted a lot of publicity and
interest. It seems everything this man touches
turns to gold. Come to think of it, don't wait to
be invited to lunch, invite him! Put it down to
expenses.'

Hannah chuckled. Mike had to be the most
exuberant member of the firm, but she couldn't
remember him ever being this excited about a
client.

'Who is this fellow, for goodness' sake?' She added teasingly, 'Superman?'

'The real world calls him Alex Drummond.' Mike hurried to the door and opened it. 'Don't forget to smile!'

Hannah's hands trembled as she opened the file. Alex Drummond's name stared up at her in big bold print. She rose from her desk and ran out to the corridor just in time to see the lift doors closing on Mike. She looked quickly up and down the long corridor. There had to be someone other than herself available to deal with Alex—there just simply had to be. She practically ran up to the receptionist's desk. 'Quick, Mary. Who's not on lunch or with a client or expecting a client during the next half-hour or so?'

The startled receptionist ran a finger down a neatly typed schedule on her desk. 'There's just one.'

Hannah almost fainted with relief. 'Who is it?' 'You?'

'Oh, lord!' She ran back to her office, shut the door and leaned against it. Alex on his way here, expecting to see Mike, getting herself instead. He would be furious. Even the most reasonable of clients felt offended if they were passed on to someone else, but to be passed on to a person you had ordered off your property would seem like the ultimate insult.

Ordered off his property! She had been able
to think of little else since that dreadful weekend.
Every detail was etched indelibly in her mind—
the fierce response when she had told him she
thought Bartholomew might be headed for
trouble and the punishing kiss in his lounge-
room. Her hand went up to her mouth in an un-
conscious gesture. If only she hadn't responded
the way she had Alex mightn't have thought so
badly of her. If only she had resisted, even a
little... But she hadn't. She had been like putty
in his hands, an eager participant.

She had never, ever responded to any man like
that, not even with men she had dated for
months. She hadn't known such physical at-
traction was possible, that there could be such
an explosive sexual reaction between two people.
She had heard of such things, of course, and
while she had thought it must be terribly exciting
she had never actually believed it. But she most
certainly did now. Her cheeks burned with remembered shame and passion.

And remembered hurt! How could Alex believe that she could be so callously cruel as to try
to get a young boy in trouble in an effort to gain
his attention? She still smarted at the way he had
ushered her out of his home and ordered one of
his workers to drive her down to her car and to
see that she left the property immediately. She
had felt like a culprit, a criminal, and tears had

stung her eyes. Tears which to her horror Alex had seen and which had only managed to harden the look in his cold, angry eyes.

Hannah cleared her head of all these thoughts. She had to get a hold on herself. When Alex walked through that door he would see a smart young solicitor standing by her desk waiting to receive him. She would be extremely businesslike, almost to the point of briskness. Yes, briskness—she liked the sound of that.

She opened the door of her small cupboard and checked her appearance in the long, narrow mirror tacked to the inside of the door. Her grey pin-striped suit was excellent. She certainly looked businesslike, but the soft rose silk blouse she wore underneath kept her from appearing brisk, which was a shame. She reached for a packet of scented wipes from the top shelf, swiftly removed her make-up and applied fresh. Next she brushed her loose flowing hair and stepped back to survey the results. Her tawny eyes sparkled with a feverish excitement and the soft blush on her cheeks wasn't the result of any make-up. Satisfied with herself, Hannah closed the door and cast a critical eye around her office.

She could find no fault there. It was as neat as a pin. Her desk was clear, apart from Alex Drummond's files, and a small crystal vase filled with pink roses. And her lunch apple. She tucked it into her top drawer and sat down to study the

files. It wouldn't do not to be thoroughly briefed
on his affairs.

Her eyes widened as she worked her way swiftly
through the sheets. No wonder Mike had insisted
that Alex Drummond be treated royally. The man
had enormous wealth. The sale of his well
equipped aeronautical engineering plant, plus
several newly constructed planes, had given him
millions. He owned vast tracts of valuable industrial land in Sydney and several more in
Brisbane. There were beach homes in Sydney's
exclusive North Shore, all rented out, plus several
large businesses, all leased, adding to his already
massive fortune. Hannah began to suspect that
the Garden Centre had been built merely as a
hobby and to provide a fantastic playground for
his nieces and nephew.

She came to the section devoted to the trust
funds. They were, as she had suspected, for the
three children. Three *wealthy* children. Their fu-
tures were assured. She placed the documents
Alex was to sign on top and closed the files. Seconds later she heard the unmistakable sound of
the lift. She stood up, took several deep, steadying
breaths, crossed the floor, opened the door and
prepared to meet the man who had ordered her
off his property. The man whose very name was
sufficient to send her pulses racing and her body
burning with a feverish shame of excitement.

She stepped into the corridor. Alex was standing in front of the receptionist's desk. Her heart stood still. He was devastatingly handsome in a light beige suit and crisp white shirt, the whiteness further enhancing his deep tan and raven-black hair. There was an unmistakable look of irritation on the rugged features as the receptionist explained the change to his appointment. Hannah walked up to the desk.

'Thank you, Mary.' She glanced up at Alex. 'My office is just down here.'

His blue eyes widened in amazement, then narrowed almost immediately into suspicious dark slits. 'You!' he snarled. 'You're the Miss Baker I'm to see?'

'Yes.' A deep flush had spread across her cheeks, caused partly by the less than friendly manner in which Alex had greeted her and the open-mouthed curiosity of the receptionist. 'If you'll just follow me, please.'

She turned and coolly walked down the corridor to her office, certain he would refuse to follow. When she heard the angry steps behind her, her heartbeats quickened. He grabbed her arm at the door, and she was forced to look up at the liquid fire burning in his eyes. 'What's going on here?' he rasped angrily. 'Where's Thompson?'

'The receptionist has already explained to you, Mr Drummond. Mr Thompson was called out unexpectedly on urgent business.'

'*My* business is urgent,' he snapped. 'If Thompson couldn't make it, he should have arranged an alternative date.'

'I'm sure he would have, but there wasn't time. You would have already been on your way and——'

'Nonsense! He could have reached me on my car phone.'

'Yes, I suppose he might have, but since you would have been practically on our doorstep he probably thought the sensible thing to do was to allow you to keep your appointment, thereby sparing you the inconvenience of making the journey twice.'

His dark face fused with anger. 'And I suppose he also thought it was only sensible to turn my affairs over to *you*?'

An angry flush stained Hannah's cheeks. 'I'm afraid he didn't have much choice in the matter.'

'You coerced him into it, no doubt,' he growled.

'I was the only one available,' Hannah managed quietly, with dignity.

'That doesn't surprise me,' he stated pompously. 'Not many people would feel comfortable trusting their affairs to a female.'

'I was the only one available,' Hannah repeated with surprising calmness, 'because this happens to be my lunch-hour.' She looked pointedly down at the hand still holding her arm. Alex followed her glance. His fingers tightened momentarily, sending another shiver of excitement coursing through her veins before he slowly released her. She stepped into her office and turned to face him. He was leaning against the door, hands jammed into the pockets of his trousers, a brooding expression on his face.

'You have a choice, Mr Drummond,' she said softly. 'You can leave, or you can come in and sign these documents.'

The stormclouds deepened and darkened on his face while a nerve thumped spasmodically along the hard line of his jaw. Hannah held her breath, wishing she had also held her tongue. If Alex walked away she knew he would never come back. The firm would have lost their most valuable client, and the fault would be hers. She could lose her position, sacked on the spot. Clients of Alex Drummond's status were few and far between. They were to be treated with velvet gloves, pampered and smiled at, no matter how rude or caustic their remarks. She thought of her mortgage payments and how long it might take before another firm hired her. She forced a smile on her face and hoped it wasn't as stiff as it felt.

'Are you always this impertinent with clients, Miss Baker?' Alex demanded.

Hannah swallowed her pride. 'I'm sorry if that's how I sounded, Mr Drummond, but believe me, that's not what I intended. I was only——'

'Thinking of your lunch-hour!' He pushed himself away from the door and entered her office. Immediately the room dwindled in size. His height, his stature, indeed his very presence seemed to consume every inch of space, soak up the oxygen and replace it with something else. Her office was suddenly *electrified*, and Hannah felt its force.

His eyes briefly scanned the room, and she felt a thrill of pride. After all, not only was the great man standing on her turf but it was also a very nice office. And she had made it even nicer with her own personal touches—the flowers for one and the two framed landscapes of Australia's ruggedly beautiful outback, the rich, earthy colours matching the curtain on her window. While her desk wasn't exactly large, it wasn't one of your standard, run-of-the-mill office types constructed from laminated wood. No, indeed. Hers was genuine mahogany. The two chairs facing it were a smart beige and deeply cushioned. The one behind her desk was much larger, almost like a throne, and when Hannah had first sat in it she had felt like a queen.

'Would you like some coffee before we get started?' she asked politely. 'Our coffee is very nice—freshly percolated.'

'No, thanks,' he answered curtly, and looked at the file on her desk. He removed a gold fountain pen from his inside pocket and, without waiting to be invited, sat down on one of the smart beige deeply cushioned chairs, nothing in his face to suggest he was impressed by its comfort.

Not that Hannah expected him to comment, of course. But sometimes people did, and she had always thought it was rather nice of them. She took her own place behind the desk and looked at him grandly across the shining, smooth surface of the mahogany.

She was in control here. He *needed* her expertise. It felt absolutely delicious having the upper hand. Already she could feel the stings and bruises starting to heal from the sharp barbs he had flung at her last weekend. She reached for the file and carefully removed the documents.

'I'll go over these with you,' she began importantly, 'to make certain you understand the conditions before you sign.'

'Not only do I understand the conditions, Miss Baker, I *made* them!' He stretched out an arrogant hand. 'The documents, please.'

Hannah handed them to him. 'Well, if you have any questions . . .' Her voice trailed off. He wasn't listening. His eyes skimmed rapidly over the pages, dark head bent in concentration as he examined the various clauses outlining the conditions of the trusts. Satisfied, he duly scrawled his signature across the dotted lines, withdrew a cheque-book and made out the amount. He slid the document back to Hannah and stood up. Her heart sank. The appointment was over. Despite his dislike for her, his arrogance and obvious annoyance that she had been thrust upon him, she had wished the appointment could have lasted forever.

She rose from her chair, which somehow no longer felt like a throne. 'It was a pleasure doing business with you, Mr Drummond,' she said in a coolly detached professional tone which gave no hint of her internal feelings. 'How... how are the children?'

'You mean have they recovered from the upset you caused them?' Alex asked caustically.

He was deliberately baiting her, but Hannah wisely held back the sharp retort hovering on her lips. She was genuinely concerned about the children, and more than once they had crowded her thoughts. 'I mean, are they well?' She added softly as though talking to herself, 'There's so much pain in Bartholomew's eyes. And dear little Josephine... so thin and nervy, as though she's waiting for something dreadful to happen. And Annabelle...' A trace of a smile lifted the corners of her mouth. 'All that make-up, and…and those clothes!'

Alex's eyes seemed to bore into hers, and time stood still as she felt herself imprisoned in their shimmering blue haze. Slowly he leaned towards her and placed his hands on the corners of her desk. Hannah's breath caught in her throat and she stifled a gasp. His face was drawn into a marble effigy of contempt, and when he spoke the silky softness of his voice was much more terrifying than had he shouted.

'Now that I know you're employed here, now that I know you've had access to my files, Miss Baker, I now consider what you did last weekend an even lowlier deed!' His eyes raked her stricken face and his mouth twisted with bitter resentment. 'When I first laid eyes on you,' he continued softly, 'I thought you were an angel. You're an angel, all right.' He pushed himself away from the desk and straightened his powerful shoulders. 'A dark angel. The devil's mistress!'

With painful realisation Hannah knew what he meant. Alex Drummond believed she was after his millions! The breath left her lungs with a sharp hiss and her hands tightly gripped the edge of the desk. He stood watching her, a cruel smile slicing his arrogant features, a cold bitterness in his eyes. Abruptly he turned and strode towards the door. It was all too much for Hannah.

'*Mr Drummond*!' she cried out, her voice charged with emotion. He turned slowly, black brows raised imperiously that she should have the audacity to address him so. Hannah flew from behind her desk and swept towards him, hardly aware of her feet touching the floor. She was consumed with a blind fury, a whirlwind concoction of anger, hurt and humiliation. She stood in front of him, her body quivering, her breathing irregular, her eyes the colour of molten lava.

'You might have great wealth, Alex Drummond, but as far as I'm concerned you're a very poor man. A man who has a stone for a heart. Not a rock, a stone, a . . . a *pebble*!'

She raised her small fists and pummelled his chest. Alex grabbed her hands into one of his own. 'Have you anything to add to that, Miss Baker?' he demanded coldly.

'Yes!' she hissed. 'I couldn't possibly be the devil's mistress. In order for that to happen, I'd have to be *your* mistress!'

An electric silence followed her words. His eyes narrowed and darkened at the fragile beauty of the heart-shaped face tilted towards his own. Hannah could smell the tantalising scent of his cologne and she could feel the warmth of his hard lean body as he drew her against him.

'And would you like that to happen, Miss Hannah Baker?' he asked softly. He drew her closer still, and fresh colour scorched her cheeks.

She stared helplessly up at him, hating him, loathing him, wanting him...!

'I c-couldn't think of a worse fate,' she husked the lie.

Her answer seemed to please him and his eyes glittered with a cold satisfaction. 'But an interesting fate all the same.' He dipped his dark head and drew her bottom lip into his mouth, and Hannah gasped as he bit lightly on the tender morsel. His hands moved slowly, sensually down her body and came to rest on her slender hips. 'I'd pay you, of course. You'd like that. The amount would depend on what we do...' he whispered against her throbbing lips as his hands pressed her into his lean hardness '...and how much pleasure we can give each other.'

He drew back his head, and Hannah knew, without doubt, that the eyes which gleamed down at her were the eyes of the devil himself. His dark lips parted in a dazzling white smile. 'And naturally you'd be at my beck and call, my slave, you might say, and I would be your master. An extremely demanding master!' The cruel contempt in his eyes sent fresh shock waves over her body. 'Well, what do you say, Hannah? Do we have a deal? Exchange money for passion?'

Hannah's answer shocked them both. The slap seemed to reverberate endlessly around the four walls of her small, neat office. She stared up at him, golden eyes rounded in horror at what she had done.

Alex raised his hand and touched his cheek. Blue fire danced dangerously in his eyes and for several terrifying seconds Hannah thought he might return the punishment.

'I'll remember this,' he drawled, 'when I have you in my bed!'

CHAPTER FOUR

HANNAH stared at the door that Alex had closed quietly behind him. She was a study in misery. He had provoked her, of course. No court in the land would condemn her action. But she condemned herself. It seemed such a shabby act. She looked at her hand. The palm was mottled and there was a twinge in her wrist. It must have hurt him. Despite her self-condemnation this realisation gave her a perverse jolt of pleasure, especially when she remembered the look of shock in those dazzling blue eyes.

But to strike a client! She shook her head in despair. Unforgivable! If word ever got around... She stirred uneasily in her throne-like chair. Should she tell Mike? *No! He would naturally want to know why*. And what would, could she say? That she had practically begged to become Alex Drummond's mistress but hadn't agreed on his terms so thought she should let him know this by delivering a hefty blow? Hannah leaned her elbows on her desk and held her head in her hands. What a mess!

The buzzer sounded on her intercom. It was Mary announcing her next appointment. A young couple were ushered in to sign mortgage documents. The chirpy brunette was in the middle stages of her pregnancy, and her sandy-haired husband beamed on her with pride. They were obviously happy, and Hannah found herself wondering what their courtship might have been like.

Had his merest touch sent the young woman's pulses racing? Had the brush of his lips against hers sent her heart skittering wildly across her chest? Had she ever found it necessary to *slap* him? No, of course not. Only Hannah Baker did such things, she thought ruefully.

As Hannah guided them through the documents she was suddenly engulfed by an overwhelming sense of loneliness. This could be me, she thought. I could be the one signing these papers with a dutiful husband at my side and a child soon to be born. She was, after all, twenty-seven years old. But she had turned down three marriage proposals over the years, and with a feeling of shock she realised they had come from men similar in nature and personality to the young man sitting at her desk.

And why had she turned them down? Because she hadn't felt the magic of a thumping heart, the frantic race of a pulse, nor the desire to slap an arrogantly handsome face with dazzling blue eyes which had the power to draw her into his very soul!

Hannah spent the remainder of the afternoon at Juvenile Court. This was the favourite part of her work, but the one which caused a great deal of sorrow. Young girls and boys, many of them not much older than Bartholomew, were seemingly bent on a course of self-destruction. By five that afternoon four teenagers had been sent to a detention centre located in the heart of Brisbane's industrial area. Hannah had visited the centre more times than she cared to remember, and she was always left with a feeling of anger, laced with hopelessness that something better couldn't be found for these sad, lonely and wayward teenagers other than the depressing grey stone building, surrounded with concrete and barbed wire fencing, which was meant to reform them.

As Hannah found her way through the heavy five o'clock traffic towards her office she thought of the heartbroken mother who had flung her arms around her defiant daughter and begged the judge to give her girl another chance. But most of the time the children were on their own, offspring of parents who had either given up on them or hadn't cared enough in the first place. Tears stung Hannah's eyes as they always did at such remembered scenes, and, although Mike had told her she would get used it, she hadn't, nor did she believe she ever would.

Mike was sitting in her office waiting for her when she returned. 'How did it go?' he asked immediately, and she knew he meant with Alex Drummond and not her afternoon in court.

'Very well,' she lied, and placed her briefcase on the floor beside her desk.

'He wasn't upset about not seeing me?'

'Perhaps a little.' That's an understatement, she thought.

'But you explained?'

'Yes, and after a while he settled down and signed the documents.' She crossed to her filing cabinet, withdrew Alex's file and handed it to Mike, glad to be rid of it.

He quickly leafed through it. 'There's a signature missing!'

'There couldn't be.'

'There is . . . right here, page five, clause three.'

Hannah looked at the page and her heart sank. There was a signature missing all right.

'Didn't you go through each page with him?' Mike asked frowningly. 'It's so easy for someone to miss a place if it's not pointed out to him.'

'I know, and I tried, but he insisted on doing it himself.'

Mike's frown deepened. 'This won't do, Hannah. It makes us appear incompetent.' He rose from his chair and sighed. 'It was bad enough having to pass him over to you, and now this!'

'I'm sorry, Mike, I really am, but he did insist——'

'And we can't very well drag him down here again,' he continued as though she hadn't spoken. Suddenly his eyes brightened. 'You live near him!' He thrust the file into her hands. 'Stop at his place on your way home. Explain what happened, throw on the charm and get his signature.'

Hannah stared at him. 'I couldn't possibly!'

'Why not?'

Because he ordered me never to set foot on his property again, that's why not! Aloud she said, 'It might seem like an imposition.'

'Nonsense! He'll be impressed by the personal attention.'

Hannah seriously doubted this. 'Couldn't we send it by courier in the morning?' she asked hopefully.

'We could...but we won't. I want to start processing by nine. The courier wouldn't get it back to me until probably lunchtime, maybe later. And if Drummond's tied up, or can't be located, it could be late in the afternoon or even the next day.'

Hannah looked miserably down at the file in her hands. There seemed no escape.

'Come on, Hannah,' scolded Mike. 'Don't look so glum. You've been uncharacteristically careless, and now you can make amends. Besides, most women would jump at the chance to spend a bit of time with Alex Drummond.'

'Uncharacteristically careless . . . make amends...jump at the chance'! Hannah's cheeks burned. She'd had enough of insufferable male arrogance for one day. She grabbed her shoulder-bag and shoved the file into her briefcase. If Alex Drummond refused her entry then so be it.

It was dusk when she arrived at the grand old homestead. The last of the setting sun caught the bougainvillaeas and cast rosy hues against the french doors and wide verandas. The lawns sweeping up to the majestic white dwelling were a rich dark green and expertly manicured. Hannah walked up the steps, and she wasn't at all surprised that her hand trembled as she lifted it to bang the brass knocker centred on the huge cedar door.

Annabelle answered. She was wearing a smart blue and white school uniform and held a large piece of chocolate cake in her hand.

'Hi, Annabelle,' Hannah greeted her warmly. 'How are you this evening?' She made her voice playfully formal because she knew Annabelle appreciated such formalities.

But not tonight, however. Annabelle took a frighteningly huge bite of her cake and skilfully narrowed her baby blue eyes. 'What are you doing here?' she demanded to know. 'I thought my uncle told you to get lost . . . and to stay lost!'

'Annabelle, don't be rude,' came the gentle voice of her sister as Josephine joined them at the door. She looked enquiringly up at Hannah and in her eyes Hannah saw a faint gleam of suspicion. 'Are you here to see Uncle Alex?' she nevertheless asked politely.

'Because if you are, you can't!' Annabelle broke in gleefully. 'Because he's not here, he's in Brisbane, and he won't be back until tomorrow or even next week, maybe even next month.'

'Annabelle, you know that's not true,' Josephine chided her gently. She offered Hannah the faintest of smiles. 'It's true he's in Brisbane, but he should be back shortly, probably in an hour or so.'

'And that's far too long to wait, in case you're thinking you might,' Annabelle decided, and started to close the door.

Hannah grabbed it firmly. 'I don't mind waiting,' she assured them with a smile. 'I need your uncle's signature on a document.'

The uneasy glances exchanged by the two sisters weren't lost on Hannah. Something was amiss here, and as Bartholomew hadn't made an appearance, she had a suspicion their concern was about him. They reluctantly allowed her to enter and Hannah followed them through to the kitchen.

The kitchen was anyone's dream and had obviously been renovated. The walls were a rich warm pine and complemented the pale blue floor tiles. Matching soft blue counter-tops seemed to

stretch endlessly, along with hordes of cup-
boards. An enormous chopping-block had pride
of place in the centre of the room and encased
six gleaming electric burners and a built-in oven.

Swooping above the electric burners was a
magnificent beaten copper hood designed, she
was sure, to eliminate even the tiniest bit of grease
or wisp of smoke. Every imaginable labour-
saving device, from a dishwasher to an auto-
matic dispenser of ice cubes set in the door of a
family-size refrigerator, had been incorporated
into the design. Hannah had seen some pretty
impressive kitchens, but this one topped them all.

'This is great!' she said admiringly as she continued to glance around, discovering new marvels
at every turn.

Her eyes stopped at the dirty dishes piled on
top of the dishwasher. 'I'll bet you're glad you
don't have to wash those,' she said kiddingly.
'You just need to pop them into the dishwasher.'

'Mrs Buckley does that,' Annabelle informed
her as she and Josephine stood rigidly on the
other side of the kitchen watching her with their
big blue eyes.

'Where is Mrs Buckley?' asked Hannah.

'She's gone home,' Josephine answered in her
soft, hesitant voice.

'But doesn't your uncle insist she stay until he
returns?'

'We told her to go,' Annabelle stated. 'We don't like her. She's so fussy, she makes us nervous.'

Hannah suppressed a smile. She couldn't imagine Annabelle allowing anyone to make her nervous. 'Well, I don't think your uncle Alex will be very pleased to learn you're here on your own,' she said.

'He won't know unless you tell him.'

'No one will need to tell him,' Hannah replied patiently. 'He'll see Mrs Buckley isn't here when he returns.'

'We always say she just left,' Josephine explained a trifle guiltily.

Hannah shook her head and sighed. 'That's really very naughty of you.' And terribly irresponsible of the housekeeper, she added silently. 'Where's Bartholomew?'

'He's...' Josephine looked helplessly at her little sister. Annabelle came to her rescue.

'He's at a friend's place,' she answered glibly. 'Doing homework,' she added for good measure.

'And we'd better get stuck into ours,' Josephine announced. They hurried away, leaving a bemused Hannah behind. She glanced up at the kitchen clock. No doubt Bartholomew would arrive moments before his uncle and Alex would assume all was well on the home front.

'Kids and uncles!' she muttered, and began stacking the dishwasher. The remains on the plates revealed that the children had dined on hot dogs. Hot dogs and chocolate cake—just what growing children needed. 'Kids and uncles,' she muttered again, and gave a rueful toss of her head.

Hannah had just finished wiping the last of the crumbs from the counter-tops when Bartholomew opened the screen door and stepped inside the kitchen. He didn't immediately see her, and she caught a glimpse of the naked misery so clearly etched on his boyishly handsome features. He looked as though he personally carried the weight of the world on his young shoulders. When he did see her, his face paled and his mouth tightened. He glanced swiftly around the huge kitchen, and Hannah knew he expected to see Alex.

'Your uncle isn't home yet,' she hastened to assure him, and immediately felt like a conspirator while wondering what lay in the child's heart to make him look so miserable.

'I'm waiting for him,' she continued, answering the unspoken question resting so suspiciously in his eyes. 'I need his signature on a document.'

'What sort of document?' She was stunned by the fear in his voice. 'Are you getting him to send me away...to one of those boys' homes?'

'Why, of course not!' Hannah answered in astonishment.

Huge tears loomed in his eyes, and he hastily brushed them away. Hannah started towards him, wanting to comfort him, to put her arms around those poor quivering shoulders, but he darted past her and shouted, 'It's all your fault! You started this!'

She stood motionless as she listened to his sneakers bounding up the stairs. And then she heard another sound—a car pulling up to the garage beyond the kitchen. She ran to the window. A sleek and very expensive silver-grey Mercedes sports convertible had just been parked. Alex slid his long legs on to the tiled driveway before reaching into the Mercedes to retrieve an attaché case and his jacket. He hadn't seen Hannah's Volvo parked at the front, shadowed by the night.

He strode briskly up to the house and entered the kitchen through the same screen door Bartholomew had only moments earlier. His eyes widened slightly at the sight of Hannah standing by the table. She had thought he would be more surprised than he appeared to be. His dark hair was ruffled by the breeze from the open convertible and his jacket was tossed casually over one broad shoulder. He looked healthy and handsome and virile, and she gave a silent pleaful prayer that her thoughts weren't revealed in her eyes.

He stood looking at her while her heart somersaulted in her chest. She met his gaze evenly, and he couldn't help but admire her nerve. She looked as fresh and as beautiful as she had earlier when he had met her in her neat little office. His eyes lingered on hers before dropping to the soft, sensuous curve of her mouth and then up again. At last he spoke.

'Well,' he drawled, 'not only are you impertinent but disobedient as well.'

'Actually, you can add one more to your list.' She took a deep breath before saying the dreadful word. 'Incompetent.'

His brows shot up in mock horror. 'Not incompetent *too*!'

A deep flush stained her smooth cheeks. 'Yes.' She resisted adding, *Thanks to you*.

'And is the object of your...incompetence...in there?' he enquired with an amused glance at her briefcase held like a shield against her chest.

'It is.'

'Then shall we go into my study to deal with it?'

Hannah hesitated. He had made his study sound like a very intimate place. The big, homey kitchen seemed so much safer.

'We could do it in here,' she hedged. 'It won't take long.' She placed her briefcase on the table.

'No, let's do it properly.' Alex picked it up with one hand and indicated his attaché case held with the other. 'After all, briefcases and attaché cases belong in a study, don't you think?'

Hannah didn't know what to think. This wasn't working out the way she had thought it would. She had expected anger, annoyance, berating, anything other than this smooth game of cat and mouse he was so obviously enjoying.

'I . . . I guess so,' she answered lamely, and followed him through a brick archway leading into an enormous dining and family room, furnished with sofas, matching chairs, coffee and end tables, the long dining table and plenty of lamps and stools. But still it looked cold and empty. There were no pictures on the bare walls, no carpets on the floor, no wood in the yawning grate of the fireplace. There was nothing to suggest that the little family spent time here . . . no books, no magazines, no toys . . . just a cold, empty room, in a cold, empty house. Hannah wondered if Mrs Buckley mightn't be responsible. Everything was spotless . . . too spotless. Perhaps the children weren't allowed to really relax. Maybe that was why Mrs Buckley made them nervous, as Annabelle had so eloquently suggested.

Alex opened the door to his study and switched on a light. Instantly the room was bathed in a warm glow. This was a man's room, most definitely. The walls were a rich red cedar and one whole wall was lined with shelves holding massive volumes of books. A beautifully aged oriental rug squared the highly polished floor. There were framed prints of aeroplanes of every imaginable shape and design. French doors lay open to the soft tropical breeze and outdoor lighting splashed on to lush greenery which partially veiled the swimming-pool and surrounding terrace. Alex indicated a chair for Hannah to sit, and as she relaxed into its comfort he walked over to an enormous antique mahogany desk which supported a computer, a brass lamp and several leather-bound books. He laid the briefcase and attaché case on its smooth surface and turned to Hannah.

'Would you like a drink?' he asked in a deeply pleasant voice.

Too pleasant. Hannah eyed him suspiciously and then her expression cleared. Perhaps he had realised he had treated her unfairly and wanted to make amends. Well, Hannah Baker certainly wasn't one to hold a grudge. She erased his slate clean and returned his smile.

'A sherry would be nice.'

She watched with glowing eyes as he walked over to a well stocked drinks cabinet and poured a sherry for her and a Scotch for himself. He had loosened the tie at his neck and the top button of his shirt was undone. Her heart melted in her chest. He was so disgustingly handsome, so totally male. A sigh escaped her lips, and he looked up at the sound and caught the un-

guarded expression in the gold hue of her eyes.
For several breathtaking seconds he held her gaze,
and Hannah was aware of a warm flush charging
through her body at the total intimacy of it all.
With enormous difficulty she managed to drag
her eyes from his and fix them safely on a huge
painting dominating the wall above the mantel
of an elaborately carved fireplace. She stared at
it for several seconds before realising who it was,
and then a sharp gasp tore from her throat.

She leaned forward in her chair. The light was
very dim on that side of the room. Hannah rose
and walked over to stand in front of it. The
children weren't much younger, and there was no
mistaking them. They stood behind their parents,
Bartholomew flanked by his two younger sisters.
The parents were seated on deeply polished high-
back chairs.

Hannah studied them. The father was dressed
in a dark business suit and could have been Alex,
so close was the resemblance. But the chin was
weak rather than strong, the mouth soft, hinting
at self-indulgence, and he wasn't nearly as
powerfully built.

Their mother was stunningly beautiful. Blue-
black hair framed a startling white complexion
dramatically emphasised by the use of mascara
and brilliant red lipstick. A smart royal-blue dress
perfectly matched the colour of her eyes.

Hannah looked at the children again. The girls wore identical white frocks, pretty on Annabelle and suitable for her age but doing absolutely nothing for Josephine other than making her appear awkward and self-conscious. Bartholomew looked handsome in a navy blue school blazer, maroon tie, white shirt and grey flannels. There was no sign of weakness in the young jaw and the blue eyes seemed steady. Alex joined her by the mantel and for several moments they viewed the picture in total silence before he said, 'It was framed just three days before the accident!'

A chill swept through her and she shivered. 'How dreadfully sad.'

'I keep it in here because it upsets the children to look at it. My study's out of bounds to them.'

'What made you decide to take the children?' she asked quietly, thinking it must have taken some considering before a bachelor took on such a responsibility, especially one as busy as Alex.

'I was the only one suitable,' he replied without hesitation. 'Both sets of grandparents are too old, and Clare's sister Hilda, while pleasant and charming, can barely take care of herself, let alone three children.' He sighed deeply. 'She's an actress.'

Hannah had to smile. The sigh and the tone seemed to express it all. 'Is it Hilda who gives Annabelle those costumes and make-up?'

Alex grimaced. 'It is!'

Hannah chuckled. 'Does she visit them often?'

'No, she hasn't been as yet, but the girls spent a week of their holidays with her in Sydney. Hilda's good to them and with them, but a week here and there is really all she could cope with. Her lifestyle is rather flamboyant, to say the least, and she spends much of her time travelling, chasing scripts...and husbands! I think she's managed to get herself married and divorced at least three times.'

Hannah's eyes sparkled with amusement. 'Auntie Hilda sounds like a pretty colourful character. I'd like to meet her some day.'

Her eyes had swept up to the painting again and so she missed seeing the hardness which had crept into Alex's eyes at her mention of meeting Hilda some day. She was studying Bartholomew's grave little face. 'Why didn't Bartholomew go with the girls to visit their aunt?' she enquired curiously.

'He preferred to stay here.'

Hannah shot him a startled glance. His voice held a chill which hadn't been present before and his eyes were narrowed on her face.

'We were putting in the lakes and dams,' he continued in that same frosty tone, 'and constructing the bridges and outbuildings. Bartholomew was rather fascinated with it all.

He's got a sharp mind. He understands the complexities of engineering.'

'Perhaps he takes after you,' Hannah murmured, bewildered that their easy rapport had lost its warmth.

Alex turned sharply on his heel and strode purposefully towards the desk. Despair washed over her. What had she *said*, what had she *done*? She had felt so ... so *close* to him, standing here discussing the children and their aunt.

He indicated her briefcase. 'Well, shall we get on with it?' he asked with a snap.

'Yes, of course.' Hannah squared her shoulders and went over to the desk. Her hands trembled as she picked up the briefcase and unlocked it. She was uncomfortably aware of those glittering blue eyes piercing her face. Her slender fingers were suddenly clumsy as she removed the document, and the cursed thing slipped through them and landed with a soft plop on to the desk. She quickly retrieved it, feeling the flush on her face growing hotter by the second.

'There's a signature missing,' she began, trying desperately for a calm, self-assured dignity to mask the fierce tenseness she was feeling by the close scrutiny of those penetrating deep blue eyes. 'Here, on ...' She frantically flicked through the pages.

'Page five, clause three!' Alex snapped impatiently.

'Th-thank you,' Hannah whispered gratefully, and her frozen fingers started to find the appropriate page, when suddenly the flush drained from her face and she looked up at him with disbelieving eyes. 'How——?'

And then everything fell into place. She might have known Alex Drummond was far too astute to miss a signature on this or any other document placed before him. His mild show of surprise at finding her in his kitchen was because, as he had said, she was disobedient. He had of course expected to confront her in her or, worse, Mike's office, when the signature was found to be missing. But why? Surely not to get her into trouble? He wouldn't stoop so low. Or would he? Her eyes narrowed on his disgustingly handsome face. And he had been so *nice* to her, actually pleasant, offering her the sherry and chatting about the children as if she were a friend instead of the foe he had made her out to be. And she had gone along with it, eagerly allowing herself to be taken in by his charm, warming to his smile and ogling at him as if he were some sort of god. He had been playing with her, toying with her, leading her into a false sense of security while knowing all along what lay in her briefcase. And it was only after she had foolishly said she would like to meet Auntie Hilda that everything had changed. He had seen it as a presumption, of course. Well, she certainly wasn't going to add to his pleasure by showing him how upset she was. Upset be damned! She was *furious*! Instead, she swallowed the sharp retorts sizzling on her lips and actually managed a smile while handing him a pen. He ignored it and took out his gold fountain pen.

'If you'd been half as interested in doing your job properly as you were in my assets, perhaps you'd have noticed this,' he growled as he scrawled his signature and handed her back the document.

'Perhaps,' she agreed, and still smiling put the papers back into her briefcase. 'But instead we've had all this *fun*!'

Hannah was almost at the door when he called out her name. She turned slowly, gracefully, her frozen smile still tacked carefully on to her face. She almost lost it when she saw her car keys dangling from his fingers. *Drat*!

'You'll be needing these,' he drawled.

'Yes, of course.' She made the return journey across the floor, warned herself not to snatch the keys from his hand but to simply accept them, and maybe, if she could manage it, even offer a polite 'thank you'. A *coup de grâce*!

And she would have managed, she knew, if only he hadn't taken her outstretched hand into the tingling warmth of his own, placed the keys firmly into the moistness of her palm and wrapped her fingers around them, one by one.

Somehow she found she simply couldn't take her eyes from the picture of her small, pale hand resting so *snugly*, so *perfectly*, in the huge darkness of his own. And if only she hadn't dragged her eyes up to meet the cobalt-blue of those penetrating orbs, then maybe her heart wouldn't have started pumping so fiercely and her mouth wouldn't have gone suddenly dry. She swallowed convulsively, and Alex's eyes slipped down to the tiny pulse beating frantically in her neck and she knew immediately that he was not only aware of her inner tension but also sensed that he was the cause of it. Then his expression changed to one Hannah couldn't define and his hand tightened around hers. The heat that generated in the hollow of her stomach moved swiftly to her muscles, weakening her, before charging through her veins and staining her skin a soft pink. For a moment his eyes held hers, then he lifted his free hand and ran a finger lightly down the burning curve of her cheek and across the softness of her lips. Her breath locked in her throat and she felt herself swaying dizzily against him as he somehow shifted his weight so that her body was pressed against his, her breasts flattening against his hard chest, and then there was the feel of an arm encircling her waist, holding her against the long lean length of his body as his hand moved up to rest just beneath the tantalising swell of her breast.

Hannah's head fell back and her lips parted in a shameless gesture of invitation. His mouth brushed the fiery lobe of her ear, moved across the silky skin of her jaw, closer and closer to the soft pink petals of her lips.

'Hannah...' He said her name in a whisper just as his mouth touched hers, and her small sigh of pleasure blended smoothly with her name. Their bodies melted together and her breast swelled into his hand. She heard his husky groan deep in his throat as his mouth moved with a savage eagerness against her own. Neither heard the soft sound the keys made as they fell on to the carpet, nor would they have cared if they had. They responded to the fierce need each had for the other, Hannah's breaths coming in short, sharp gasps as Alex's hands moved over her body in an intimacy she knew she had been craving. He moved her within his arms to deftly unbutton the small pearls of her blouse. His lips burned against the soft swell of her breasts rising above the lacy confines of her bra. She felt his lean fingers reach behind to unclasp it, and her body trembled with renewed anticipation.

'Hannah,' he said again, and she heard the raw emotion in his voice and her eyes opened slightly and through the hazy smoke of passion caught sight of the family painting. Instantly her body stiffened and she pulled herself away from him, frantically clutching at her bra and blouse, panic and self-loathing written clearly on her face and blazing from her eyes.

Alex dragged a hand roughly through his hair and said quietly, 'I'm sorry, Hannah. I didn't mean that to happen.'

'Do you honestly expect me to believe that?' she asked shakily, conveniently managing to forget that she had done nothing to prevent it. 'Especially as you orchestrated it all?'

An abrupt silence followed her words, a dreadful silence in which she found she couldn't meet his eyes as she clumsily managed to restore order to her clothing while also painfully aware of the huge painting looming above them, five sets of eyes staring down, three of them accusingly.

'Whether you accept my apology or not is entirely up to you,' Alex stated in such a quiet voice that Hannah could barely hear. Without a further word, he picked up the car keys, grabbed her briefcase from the desk, crossed the room, opened the door and waited with a cool politeness for her to pass.

CHAPTER FIVE

THE Volvo shot down the lane, rose above the crest, and Hannah caught a glimpse of Alex standing on the veranda before he disappeared from her rear-view mirror and she was hurtling down the rest of the drive and finally on to the highway. Her knuckles were white as she clutched the steering-wheel, and her mind raced with a million thoughts.

Alex had deliberately avoided putting his signature on one of the clauses, but had it been done solely to lure her to his home *to make love to her*? No! No, the rational part of herself refused to believe that. He had done it merely to teach her a lesson. And he had no way of knowing that Mike would force her to go to his home for the signature, so the lovemaking couldn't have been planned. It had just happened! And she knew he had been every bit as affected by it as she had. She could still feel the warmth of his hands where he had touched her, and her mouth throbbed from his kisses. She couldn't help but wonder just how far their lovemaking would have gone if she hadn't looked up to see the picture. A cold chill washed over her and she shivered without knowing why. There had been something about their faces . . . and she shivered again.

Warning lights ahead blinked yellow against the blackness of the night. Hannah slowed down and groaned inwardly. There was a detour ahead. She veered carefully on to the dirt track and pushed all thoughts of Alex to the back of her mind as she concentrated on the hazardous stretch of road. All she needed to really complete her day was to get bogged down, she thought grimly, or, just as wonderful, to get a flat tyre. When she finally drove into her driveway, she was mentally and physically exhausted. A warm bath, an omelette and straight to bed, she told herself as she fumbled in her bag for her house keys.

An internal noise reached her ears and made the small hairs at the nape of her neck stand on end. Suddenly she was painfully aware of the cottage's isolation and the total blackness of the night. Her frayed nerves tensed and her muscles stiffened as she awaited for another tell-tale noise. When none was forthcoming, she forced herself to relax. She had simply imagined the sound, allowing the events of the day to play havoc with her senses. She inserted the key and opened the door. As she switched on the hall light, she saw the knob of her bedroom door slowly turn and the soft click as it shut.

Someone's in there! For a few seconds, Hannah's brain became paralysed with fear and her body felt numb. The shrill of the telephone ringing jerked her to her senses. But the telephone was in the kitchen, almost across the hall from the bedroom. What if she answered it and the culprit grabbed her from behind? She had heard of that happening. Maybe she should run outside and get back into her car. No, there could be more than one intruder. The telephone continued to ring while her heart thumped wildly against her ribs. When it finally stopped she felt awash with despair. Somehow, while it rang, she had felt safe. She silently willed it to ring again.

Alex put down the telephone and stared at it with a mixture of annoyance and concern in his eyes. Hannah should have been home by now, and he wondered if she was deliberately not answering her phone. He had heard Annabelle's prayers, helped Josephine with a few tricky maths problems and had a quiet chat with Bartholomew before returning to his study with the intention of catching up with some much needed paperwork. But he had found it almost impossible to concentrate.

Hannah was on his mind. Hannah with the bewitching golden eyes and the irresistible smile which could do strange things to a man's soul. *His* soul! He got up from his desk, paced the floor a few times, flicked open a file, shut it and stared unseeingly at the green face of his computer before reaching for the phone again. This time she answered, and he knew instinctively that something was wrong. His ears had picked up the faint tremor in her voice.

'Why didn't you answer before?' he asked abruptly without any preamble.

'I...I...oh, Alex, I...I couldn't.' She rushed on, holding on to the receiver as if she was actually holding on to him. 'There was an intruder...burglars. Here, in...in my bedroom.' She laughed shakily. 'I was too frightened to *move*, and——'

'I'll be right over!'

Alex charged up the stairs. Annabelle and Bartholomew were asleep, but Josephine was sitting up in bed reading.

'I'm going out for an hour or two,' he told her. 'Security will keep watch over the house.'

'Where are you going?' she asked anxiously.

'To Miss Baker's place. She's...had a bit of trouble over there.'

'Are you worried about her?'

'I'm...concerned,' Alex admitted.

Josephine smiled. 'I thought you didn't like her.'

'That has nothing to do with it.'

'If you didn't like her you wouldn't be concerned about her,' Josephine needlessly pointed out to him.

'Perhaps you're right,' he growled. 'Now go to sleep.'

'May I finish this chapter first? It's only three more pages.'

'All right, but no more.' He watched as she settled back to her book. Hannah's right, he thought—the child is far too thin. 'Are you taking your vitamins?' he asked.

Josephine glanced up from her book and nodded. 'I very rarely forget.'

'Try never to forget.' He smiled and left her.

Alex climbed into the Rover and stopped briefly at the security hut to inform the patrol that he would be out for a while and to keep special watch over the homestead. When he arrived at Hannah's, her small cottage was lit up like a Christmas tree. She opened the door when she heard the Rover and waited for him on the step. Her face was pale and he could see she was still very upset although doing her best to hide this from him. When they were inside, he swung her gently around to face him. 'Are you all right?' he asked anxiously, and when she heard the undisguised concern in his voice her resolve broke and she found herself in his arms, clinging to him as if she would never let him go, feeling his strong, warm arms around her in a protective embrace while listening to his low reassuring voice and the steady thump of his heart against her cheek. A convulsive tremor shot through her and he held her closer still. He felt the warmth of her tears seep through his shirt and on to his chest, while her nostrils filled with the clean male scent of him. She had been terrified, but now she was safe. Alex had come, as she had somehow known he would even before he had called, just as she knew it had been him who had rung while the intruder was in the house. She was in his arms where she knew she belonged. She knew this because...*she loved him*! Oh, God, how she loved him! Her discovery both thrilled and terrified her. Thrilled her because it was the most heartrendingly beautiful feeling she had ever experienced, and terrified her because the man she loved harboured only the darkest feelings about her character. He would never return her love, but she knew he could break her heart. Hannah carefully removed herself from his arms and stepped away from him.

'Look at me,' she said as she quickly wiped away her tears. 'C-crying like a baby, for goodness' sake. I...I deal with this sort of thing every day, but I guess it's a little different when it finally happens to yourself.' Her smile was bright. Too bright.

Alex led her to the sofa and sat down beside her. He took her cold hands into his and gently massaged them. 'Have you rung the police?' he asked.

Hannah shook her head. 'No.'

'I'll do it.' He started to rise, but Hannah placed a hand on his arm.

'Please don't.'

Alex frowned down at her. 'A crime has been committed. It must be reported, Hannah.'

'There's been a crime all right, but not the type you're thinking about.' She rose and took his hand. 'I'll show you.'

She led him down the hall to her bedroom. The door was open and the light on. Her bed had been stripped bare of its blankets and pillows.

'They took your blankets?' Alex asked incredulously.

Hannah nodded. 'The nights are getting cold... and will get colder still.' She walked over to her bureau. The drawers were pulled out. Alex followed her and stared into the almost empty recesses. 'Most of my thick woollen sweaters are gone,' she said simply, and closed the drawers, one by one.

Alex was clearly puzzled. 'Didn't they take anything of *value*?'

'What could be more valuable than a warm sweater and a blanket to snuggle into on a cold night?'

'You're treating this far too lightly, Hannah,' he told her, exasperated. 'It really doesn't matter what has or hasn't been taken. What matters, is the fact that your house was broken into and you might have been harmed.'

Hannah ignored this. She reached for his hand again, and with his exasperation mounting by the second, he nevertheless allowed her to lead him into the kitchen. She opened the door of the refrigerator and stood back for him to see.

'You're out of food,' he said with a drawl.

'I am now,' she agreed, and shut the door and opened the door to the pantry. Alex wasn't in the least surprised to see the shelves empty.

' "And when she got there the cupboard was bare," ' he quoted softly. He shoved his hands into the pockets of his trousers and peered at Hannah beneath hooded lids. 'Why do I get the distinct impression that instead of being outraged at the injustice done to you, you seem actually glad, grateful even, that these things have been taken from you?'

'I'm not glad...or grateful.' She sighed heavily. 'I'm sad!'

'And well you should be!' He put his hands on her shoulders. 'The authorities must be notified, Hannah. Criminals can't be allowed to roam through neighbourhoods unchecked.'

'They're *not* criminals, Alex.'

'No?' He dropped his hands and shook his head impatiently. 'And what would you call them?'

'Children,' she answered sorrowfully.

'Children?' he repeated with a loud snort. 'Don't be ridiculous, Hannah. Children don't go around robbing people, especially at this hour of the night.'

'They'd be snug in their beds at home, you mean?' Her voice had grown cold.

'Of course.' He frowned darkly. 'I'm going to take a look outside.'

When he returned several minutes later, his face was flushed with anger. 'No wonder they were able to break in,' he stormed. 'The locks on your doors and windows are antiquated. Good grief, Hannah, haven't you any sense of security? A child with a toothpick could get in.' When he saw the look on her face he added quickly, 'Not that I believe for an instant that it was a child . . . or children.'

'You don't believe it because you don't want to,' Hannah returned quietly. 'No one likes to think of children being cold and hungry, without homes.' She looked appealingly up at him and he saw the sadness that lingered in her eyes. 'Think of what was taken, Alex. Food . . . blankets . . . clothing. Nothing else . . . and nothing was broken, no damage, no mess, just . . .'

'All right,' he sighed, 'maybe it was children. *This time*! Maybe next time you mightn't be so lucky. All your locks need replacing, and you should have grilles on your windows, an alarm system installed. You're a solicitor, for Pete's sake. Surely you should realise better than most about the ever-increasing crime rate on the Coast!'

Hannah turned away from him. Exhaustion swept over her in waves and she felt weak and defenceless. Yes, she did know better than most about the rapidly growing crime rate on the Coast and practically every town and city across the country. She also knew what most others didn't. Most of the crimes were being committed by young, homeless 'street kids' who weren't eligible for government benefits and survived solely by their wits. She felt Alex's hand on her arm and closed her eyes in an attempt to hold back the tears which were threatening to spill down her cheeks.

'Pack a bag, Hannah,' he said gruffly. 'You're coming home with me.'

She whirled to face him, her mouth opening to protest, but he held up a restraining hand, effectively silencing any argument she might broach. 'You can't stay here,' he said reasonably, 'without food or blankets.' He placed his hands on the sides of her face and tilted up her chin. There were purple smudges beneath her eyes and her skin was porcelain white. She looked about ready to collapse.

'Pack enough for a few days,' he added firmly. 'You're not coming back here until the place is properly secured.'

'But . . .'

'Don't argue with me, Hannah, I'm not in the mood. Either pack that bag or I'll do it for you.'

She knew he meant it, and besides, she simply lacked the strength to argue, knowing there was no possibility of herself emerging as the winner.

'All right,' she sighed. 'If you think it's absolutely necessary.'

'I do,' he smiled, and her breath caught in her throat as it moved up to melt in his eyes. 'Most absolutely,' he added with a drawl. His hands gently pushed the fine silky hair away from her temples. 'You'll be safe there.'

Would she? Hannah shivered at the feel of his hands smoothing back her hair and the touch of his fingers against the tender skin of her neck. It was meant to comfort, she knew, but instead it was sending shivers of delight throughout her body. She would have stayed there forever savouring the exquisite magic of his caress if he hadn't suddenly set her away from him. 'Pack your bag, Hannah,' he ordered gruffly.

And she flew to do his bidding, grabbing clothes from her wardrobe and quickly packing them into her suitcase, fearful that if she took too long he might change his mind and decide she didn't need his protection after all.

'Ready,' she announced almost breathlessly, and when Alex looked up from the lock he was examining on her lounge-room window he saw a flush had replaced the paleness of her cheeks. A slow smile spread evenly across the hard line of his mouth and exploded in her heart.

'Good.' He took the suitcase, and she picked up her shoulder-bag and briefcase before taking a last look around. When they were outside and he was leading her towards the Range Rover she asked about her car.

'I'll send someone over for it tomorrow,' he assured her, and helped her into the high seat of the Rover.

All was quiet at the graceful homestead when they arrived, and Alex escorted Hannah up the sweeping staircase. As they trod softly down the long, wide hall, Alex paused at one of the bedrooms and looked in. Immediately his expression softened and Hannah saw a fierce look of protective love flare in his eyes before he crossed the room to remove a book from the sleeping Josephine's hands, slip away one of the pillows propping her up and gently lift a blanket to cover the thin little shoulders before switching off her bedside lamp. The whole operation was over in seconds and executed with the practised ease of one who had performed this task many times before. As Hannah watched, her heart expanded even more with the love she felt for this man.

The bedroom which was to be hers was sparsely furnished with a double bed, night tables on either side, a tall bureau and a chair. There were no pictures on the walls, nor was there a carpet on the highly polished wooden floors. As in the rest of the house there was the faint lingering aroma of fresh paint and the ever-present feel of loneliness. Alex laid her suitcase on the bed, crossed the room and opened a door. Hannah could see the fresh gleam of new tiles and soon the thunder of water filling a sparkling white tub. He tested the water and adjusted the taps, and she smiled with loving approval. He wanted the temperature to be just right for her, not too hot, not too cold. He cares for me, she thought happily, and her heart soared with the thought.

Alex straightened and turned to look at her. 'The tub will fill quickly. You'd better undress.'

Hannah nodded and waited for him to leave. Instead he sent a searching glance around the bathroom, obviously looking for something he thought should be there.

'Towels?' Hannah suggested helpfully, and pointed to a rack where several lay neatly folded. 'There's plenty.'

'No... bubbles.'

'Bubbles?' Hannah repeated with a grin. 'Am I to have a bubble bath?' Her eyes glowed. 'How lovely.'

'I guess you'll have to do without,' Alex growled as he finished his search. 'There doesn't seem to be any here.' He bent down and turned off the taps. When he straightened his eyes met hers and a roaring filled her ears. His black hair fell over his wide brow, slightly dampened from the steam, and his naturally dark complexion glowed with a healthy ruddiness which only served to highlight his rugged masculinity.

'The girls must have taken it,' Hannah heard him say, and it was as if his deep voice came from a far distance.

She felt her head move as she nodded and the faraway sound of her own voice as she murmured, 'Little girls like bubble baths.'

And then he was standing right in front of her and she was gazing helplessly up at the dark mystery of his heavily lashed eyes and losing herself to the slow curve of his sensuous mouth as his lips parted in a gleaming white smile.

'And, apparently, so do big girls.' His eyes rested on the shimmering halo of her golden hair before drifting leisurely down to her face. Hannah's heart hammered in her chest. She wanted him to claim her, crush her against his hard breast, touch her, stroke her, kiss her. This desperate yearning filled her eyes and was there, naked, for him to see. He lifted a hand and her heart stood still, but instead of touching her he shoved both his hands into his pockets.

'Your bath's getting cold, Hannah,' he stated crisply, and stepped past her into the bedroom. He paused and added, 'Are you hungry?'

'For....' She swallowed hard. 'For food?'

He frowned darkly. 'Of course.'

'Well, I ... I haven't had dinner.'

His frown deepened. 'I thought as much. You must be famished.'

As though eavesdropping, her tummy chose that moment to agree loudly. Hannah's cheeks flushed with embarrassment, while Alex's features relaxed into a grin. 'That's what I thought. How does a few toasted sandwiches and a bowl of soup sound?'

Before Hannah could say 'absolutely heavenly' her tummy answered for her with another joyful rumble. Alex chuckled and left the room, leaving her to get on with her bath. She caught a glimpse of herself in the mirror. The steamy glass contorted her image and suited the way she was feeling. She looked wild. Her hair was in disarray and except for two hot spots of colour high on her cheeks her complexion was pale, making her eyes seem like two black holes in her face. She sighed heavily and went into the bedroom to get a nightdress and dressing-gown from the suitcase, stripped herself bare and sank gratefully into the soothing hot water. The fragrant soap felt good against her skin, and she lay back in the tub rubbing the bar gently over her breasts and the flat smoothness of her stomach, and all the while her thoughts were on Alex.

He had *known* she wanted him to kiss her, hold her in his arms. And for a split second she had thought he was going to answer the yearning he had surely seen in her eyes. But he had stopped

NO COST! NO OBLIGATION TO BUY!
NO PURCHASE NECESSARY!

PLAY "LUCKY 7"
AND GET AS MANY AS SIX FREE GIFTS...

HOW TO PLAY:

1 With a coin, carefully scratch off the silver box opposite. You will now be eligible to receive two or more FREE books, and possibly other gifts, depending on what is revealed beneath the scratch off area.

2 When you return this card, you'll receive specially selected Mills & Boon Romances. We'll send you the books and gifts you qualify for absolutely FREE, and at the same time we'll reserve you a subscription to our Reader Service.

3 If we don't hear from you within 10 days, we'll then send you four brand new Romances to read and enjoy every month for just £1.80 each, the same price as the books in the shops. There is no extra charge for postage and handling. There are no hidden extras.

4 When you join the Mills & Boon Reader Service, you'll also get our free monthly Newsletter, featuring author news, horoscopes, penfriends and competitions.

5 You are under no obligation, and may cancel or suspend your subscription at any time simply by writing to us.

You'll love your cuddly teddy. His brown eyes and cute face are sure to make you smile.

Play "Lucky 7"

Just scratch off the silver box with a coin.
Then check below to see which gifts you get.

YES! I have scratched off the silver box. Please send me all the gifts for which I qualify. I understand that I am under no obligation to purchase any books, as explained on the opposite page. I am over 18 years of age.

MS/MRS/MISS/MR _____ 6A3R

ADDRESS _____

_____

POSTCODE _____ SIGNATURE _____

7 7 7	**WORTH FOUR FREE BOOKS** **FREE TEDDY BEAR AND MYSTERY GIFT**
🔔 🔔 🔔	**WORTH FOUR FREE BOOKS** **AND MYSTERY GIFT**
🍒 🍒 🍒	**WORTH FOUR FREE BOOKS**
🍒 🔔 BAR	**WORTH TWO FREE BOOKS**

MILLS & BOON "NO RISK" GUARANTEE

- You're not required to buy a single book!
- You must be completely satisfied or you may cancel at any time simply by writing to us. You will receive no more books; you'll have no further obligation.
- The free books and gifts you receive from this offer remain yours to keep no matter what you decide.

If offer details are missing, write to:
Mills & Boon Reader Service, P.O. Box 236, Croydon, Surrey CR9 9EL

Mills & Boon Reader Service
FREEPOST
P.O. Box 236
Croydon
Surrey
CR9 9EL

NO
STAMP
NEEDED

himself, deliberately pulled away. *Why*? Was there someone else? This thought was too painful even to contemplate, so her mind searched for other reasons. He obviously cared for her. Why else would he have rushed over to her place when he learned she was in trouble? Of course, he could have acted out of guilt because it had been, after all, his fault that she had been so late in arriving home, a dark house an easy target for intruders.

Or maybe... maybe he simply didn't want any more commitments. The children were a big enough responsibility and each, in their own way, emotionally draining. If only the children liked her, trusted her, then maybe he would see...

There was a sharp rap on the bathroom door before it was flung open. Hannah shot up in the tub. Alex's eyes gleamed down at her, and she crossed her arms across her breasts and stared unblinkingly up at him.

'I thought you must have dozed off,' he said, and bent to run a hand through the water. 'It's cold. Why aren't you out?' He reached for her hand and she felt a tingling warmth as it brushed against the rosy tip of her nipple.

'Get me a towel,' she gasped, and shrank further back in the tub, staring down at the dark hand resting so close to her breast. Alex turned to look at the rack of towels.

'Which colour do you want?'

'It doesn't matter.'

'Well, there's blue, or green, yellow, pink, white...'

Hannah's teeth chattered and she shivered, not from the cold but because he had turned to look at her again, and try as she might she simply couldn't tear her eyes away from those penetrating, all-consuming, deep blue orbs.

'All of them,' she yelped.

His black brows rose. 'All of them?' he repeated in mock innocence.

'Y-yes.'

Alex rose from the tub and grabbed a towel from the rack. 'I think the green,' he said. 'It'll bring out the green in your eyes.' He spread it out. It was huge, and, by the way he was looking at her, Hannah knew she was expected to stand up so he could wrap it around her. Well, she wasn't about to accept this courtesy!

She stretched out her arm, keeping her other across her breasts. 'Give it to me.'

His black brows rose again in majestic splendour. 'Just...give it to me?' he repeated in mock horror. 'No, "*please, Alex*"?'

'Please, Alex,' she added stiffly.

'That's better.' He smiled and handed it to her and watched while she inched her way up out of the tub, careful to cover her sleek nakedness as she rose. 'Thank you,' she muttered when she was safely wrapped up. 'With any luck at all I should stop shivering within a month or two!'

He chuckled and opened the door, stepping aside for her to pass. Once she was inside the bedroom the tantalising aroma of hot chicken soup and toasted cheese sandwiches assailed her nostrils. Hannah sighed gratefully and the corners of her mouth dimpled into a smile as she looked up at him.

'Thank you,' she said humbly. 'It was very nice of you to... to go to so much trouble.'

'I thought so too,' he agreed easily, and she saw the devil dancing in his eyes before he wrapped a finger under her chin and lowered his head to capture her mouth beneath his own.

The kiss was long and tantalisingly slow, his lips lightly teasing, brushing and stroking her mouth until she was clinging to him, her arms wrapped around his neck, her fingers splaying wildly through the thick black scrub of his hair, tangling the wiry strands around and through them, her breathing ragged and then stopping altogether as he slipped the towel from her slender body and picked her up in his arms to carry her across to the bed.

He laid her gently down and stood above her. His passion-filled eyes held hers as he slowly removed his tie and unbuttoned his shirt before he joined her on the bed and gathered her again in his arms. 'You're so lovely, Hannah,' he whispered against her fever-flushed cheek, his lips hard and scorching against the smoothness of her neck and the roundness of her shoulder before finally claiming the throbbing erected peak of her breast. She gasped aloud as his teeth bit lightly down on the pinkened nub while his hand moved slowly over her tummy and between her thighs.

And she knew this was what she wanted, had wanted forever, and she gave in willingly to the magic of those strong brown arms crushing her against him, and she pressed her breasts eagerly into the hard wall of his chest, her mouth opened wide to receive the full thrust of his tongue, plundering her with his passion, and she eagerly welcomed such an intimate invasion. And when she felt his hand go down to the buckle of his belt and the naked hardness of his thighs cross over her, her nails dug into his powerful shoulders before her hands slipped up lovingly to capture the hardness of his cheeks, dark with the fever of his passion. Their eyes locked, and Hannah whispered with all the fervour she felt, 'I love you, Alex!' And it came straight from her heart.

'You're incredibly beautiful, Hannah,' he groaned against her cheek. His mouth started to close over hers in another searing embrace when she stiffened and turned her head away. With an agonised moan he raised himself on his elbows and looked at her with a growing harshness in his glittering blue eyes.

'Is this some sort of game of yours?' he asked thickly, and her heart shrank at the disgust she heard in his voice. 'Waiting until the last possible second and calling a halt?' He drew away from her, sitting on the edge of the bed and dragging his hands through his hair, watching as Hannah drew the sheet up to cover her nakedness.

'I . . . I'm sorry,' she whispered, her eyes softly pleading as she met the coldness in his own as he continued his silent appraisal. 'I . . . I'm not ready. I didn't think this would . . . would happen.'

But even as she said the words she knew it simply wasn't true. She had wanted it to happen because she loved him. Her only regret was in telling him so. If only she had kept those three little words to herself then maybe she wouldn't be feeling so incredibly hurt. Alex hadn't responded in kind. He had merely said she was beautiful, a meaningless utterance, probably said many times to the women he held in his arms. Fresh hurt washed over her, and she dragged her eyes from his and toyed with the sheet clutched tightly in her hands.

She felt his weight leave the bed and saw the anger in his eyes as he slowly pulled on his shirt and trousers, and she wondered if he had even heard her cry of love. Hope filled her heart. Perhaps she wouldn't feel so threatened by her emotions if she knew he hadn't. But even if he had, there must be some way to reverse her words.

'Alex,' she began shakily, and she even attempted a smile, 'when I said I loved you—well, I really didn't mean it.'

'No?'

So he *had* heard. 'No,' she sighed.

'It doesn't surprise me. You do and say a lot of things you don't mean!'

Colour flooded her cheeks. 'I guess it was because I was feeling so . . . so grateful.' At the look in his eyes she added quickly, 'Not because you were making love to me.'

'Of course not.'

'It was because you came to my rescue.'

'I hardly came to your rescue, Hannah,' he corrected drily. 'The intruders had already left by the time I arrived.'

'I know, but . . . but I was feeling a little bit scared and . . . and jumpy. I was just so grateful to see you that I guess I thought. . . .' She swallowed hard before she could continue. 'I guess I thought I loved you.' Tears burned at the backs of her eyes and she quickly lowered them.

'Look at me, Hannah.'

The sudden gentleness of his voice made her glance up quickly, to peep cautiously up at him through the golden tips of her lashes. The anger seemed to have left him and she saw something she couldn't define glinting in his eyes which somehow managed to soften the hard lines of his face.

'Yes?' she asked hesitantly.

To her astonishment he actually grinned, and it was enough to send her heart sky-rocketing up to her throat. He bent over her and pressed his forehead against hers. 'You're a terrible liar!' he whispered, and straightened again to his full height. 'Now drink your soup!'

CHAPTER SIX

HANNAH tossed and turned in her sleep. She was making a desperate dash through the woods. A young boy on a red trail bike was chasing her. She knew it was Bartholomew. As the trail bike picked up speed, her legs seemed to grow weaker. Any moment now and he would run her down.

Through a clearing in the trees she could make out the tall, dark figure of Alex. He was urging her to run faster and his hand was stretched out to her. Just when she was about to grab it he disappeared and reappeared deeper in the woods, his hand still outstretched while the bike roared closer still.

'Alex,' she sobbed. 'Alex, help me!'

'*Say please!*' His voice rumbled through the woods and struck at the trunks of the trees, lashed at the branches, slapped the leaves until finally reaching her ears.

'*Please*! *Please*! *Please*!' Hannah shot up in bed, drenched in perspiration, heart thumping wildly. 'Please,' she whispered again, and fell back against the pillows, totally exhausted. And then she heard another sound—soft moaning, mewling sounds, and at first she thought it was herself and that she was still caught up in the dreadful nightmare. She sat up and strained her ears, listening closely. A child was crying, the wretched moanings carried through the still night air to her opened bedroom windows.

She got out of bed, slipped into her pale blue robe and stepped out into the hall. Through the dark shadowy gloom of the night she saw Alex disappear into one of the children's bedrooms. Hannah hurried down the corridor and stopped at the opened door. What she saw wrenched painfully at her heart.

Alex was sitting on the edge of Bartholomew's bed, his huge hand gently stroking his nephew's brow while the child thrashed and twisted in agony, tortured by his dreams. The moonlight filtered through the windows and caught Alex's face. Hannah saw the naked misery, the grief, the pity, the love, the wretched sorrow so clearly etched on his dark features and heard his voice, oh, so gentle and tender, as he soothed the tormented child.

She stood there, frozen, unable to move, Alex's anguish reflected in her own eyes. She knew instinctively that what she was witnessing had happened many times before. When at last the child was still and had settled into a peaceful slumber, Alex remained sitting on the bed, gazing sorrowfully down at the little form. Hannah almost cried aloud at the naked grief on his face. Maybe she did make a sound, for suddenly Alex looked up, and anger flared in his eyes at the sight of her small, ghostlike figure clutching at the bedroom door, her eyes large and luminous, filled with the love she felt for him and anguished for the sorrow she knew was in his heart. He got up, crossed the room and propelled her into the hall, closing the door softly behind them.

'I'm sorry your sleep has been disturbed,' he said coldly. 'Perhaps I should have warned you that Bartholomew suffers from the occasional nightmare.'

'Alex, please, I'm not the enemy,' she said gently, her troubled eyes touching each crevice of his face. 'You look exhausted. You're still in your clothes. You haven't been to bed.' She reached up and touched his hard cheek. 'You can't go on this way.'

He took her hand and pressed it against his lips before dropping it. 'And what are you suggesting?' he asked as his eyes swept over the front of her silk nightdress not covered by the robe. 'That you want to make amends by inviting me into your bed?' He smiled coldly and shoved his hands into his pockets. 'I hate to disappoint a lady, but, as you've already observed, I'm exhausted.' He pulled out his hand and draped an arm around her slender shoulders as he led her back to her bedroom. 'My performance mightn't be up to my usual standard, but if you're willing to take a chance then what the heck, so am I.'

'You know very well that's not what I'm suggesting,' Hannah told him as she slipped discreetly away from his arm. She took a deep breath and added carefully, 'Bartholomew needs help, Alex. Professional help.'

His eyes narrowed on her face. 'You witness one bad dream,' he rasped harshly, 'and you immediately conclude that he needs help, professional help. A *psychiatrist*!'

'He's deeply troubled.'

'Of course he is! He lost his parents.'

'The accident happened a year ago. He should have begun to accept it by now, come to terms with his grief.'

Alex dragged a hand roughly through his hair and down the side of his jaw. 'He just needs more time,' he stated wearily.

'That's where a doctor can help him.' Hannah placed a gentle hand on his arm and felt the tenseness of his muscles. 'His wasn't an ordinary nightmare. He's suffering, and...and so are you.' She swallowed hard and longed more than anything to hold this proud, strong man in her arms and soothe him the way he had Bartholomew. 'And so are the girls. None...' Her voice broke, 'none of you can be happy when one of you is hurting so badly,' she finished in a hoarse whisper.

Alex gave her a long, hard look. 'Perhaps you set too much store by happiness, Hannah,' he said quietly.

He left her then, his proud shoulders slightly bent as he made his way down the darkened hallway to his bedroom. Hannah watched him go, his image blurred by the tears rising in her eyes. The old house creaked and groaned in the night, and she couldn't help but wonder if there would ever be the sounds of laughter here.

She awoke in the morning to a room filled with sunshine. She was alarmed to see that it was almost ten o'clock. Mike would be furious, waiting for the documents, wondering where in the world she could possibly be. She dressed quickly, choosing an attractive lemon-coloured dress which gently hugged the slender lines of her body. The house was quiet, not a sound to be heard. The children would be at school, of course, and Alex attending to business, but the stillness seemed somehow oppressive. She thought of Bartholomew and his dreadful nightmare and wondered how he was feeling today. He would more than likely be exhausted.

She remembered seeing a telephone in Alex's study. It would be wise to ring Mike, explain what happened and tell him she was on her way. Hannah ran down the deserted hall and skipped lightly down the stairs. Mike would probably be rendered speechless when she told him she was going to be Alex Drummond's guest for the next few days. The thought put a smile on her face, and it was still there when she flew into the study. Alex looked up from his desk.

'Usually people knock before they barge in here,' he growled.

'Oh, I'm *so* sorry!' Hannah blurted the apology. 'I didn't realise you'd be here.'

'No?' He leaned back in his chair and clasped his hands behind his head. The sunlight filtering through the opened french doors cast blue shadows across his black hair. She knew he hadn't got much sleep the night before, but still he looked fresh and immaculate, his royal-blue polo shirt enhancing his bronzed complexion and outlining the supple muscles beneath the fabric. 'Then why would you come in here?'

A hot flush soared to her cheeks at the implication in his voice. 'To use your telephone,' she answered stiffly.

'There are several scattered throughout the house.'

'I didn't know.' She turned to leave. 'I . . . I'll find one.'

'Whom did you wish to ring?'

'Mike Thompson. I'm late for work, and he'll be wondering where I am.'

'He knows where you are. I rang him first thing this morning.'

A smile of relief flashed across her delicate features. 'Thank you.'

'I also told him you're taking a week's holiday...*here*!'

The smile disappeared. 'You did *what*?'

'I explained about the burglary, and he agreed with me that you needed the time to get over the trauma.'

'What trauma?' Hannah glared at him. 'My God, you have a nerve. I've been saving up my holidays for a *cruise*!'

'Now isn't that unfortunate? I can imagine your disappointment.' Alex beamed her a smile.

'What *else* have you done?' she demanded heatedly.

'Forwarded the documents to your office, arranged to have your cottage properly secured, and your car is now parked in my garage.' He reached into the pocket of cream-coloured trousers and withdrew her keys. 'No need to thank me—I can see by the expression on your beautiful face that you're extremely grateful.'

Frustration bit at the back of her throat. She reached for the telephone. 'I'll ring Mike and tell him I'm available for emergencies and——'

'There won't be any emergencies.'

'There are *always* emergencies!' She started to dial, but Alex took the receiver from her hand and placed it back on the cradle. 'That's another thing I did,' he drawled with that same wicked smile. 'Got an assurance from Mike that you wouldn't be disturbed.' The smile kicked into a grin. 'Now wasn't that thoughtful of me?'

'You're incorrigible!' Hannah said crossly.

'And you're very beautiful.' His eyes drifted over her at a leisurely pace, filling her body with a tingling awareness. 'No executive suit today. I'm glad to see you don't always go in for power dressing.'

'Suits are more practical,' she explained.

'But not nearly as attractive.' He rose from his desk and went over to the bar. 'Would you like some coffee?'

'Yes, please.'

'And a blueberry muffin to go with it?'

'That would be very nice.'

Alex poured the coffee from a gleaming silver coffee pot into two large mugs, placed the mugs on the desk along with a plate filled with delicious-looking, plump muffins. Next he pulled up a chair and set it beside his behind the desk. Hannah viewed the whole operation with a guarded look in her eyes.

'I hope you don't expect me to sit around all day drinking coffee and eating blueberry muffins?' Her voice sounded strained and she could barely hear it over the thumping of her heart. Her eyes were glued to the chair resting so snugly against his own. She knew she would soon be sitting on it.

'Certainly not!' Alex held out the chair. 'Naturally I expect you to earn my hospitality.'

'Naturally.'

'Come and sit down.'

'Hannah hesitated. 'How...how do you expect me to earn it?' she asked.

'Well, for one thing I'd very much appreciate it if you could take the girls shopping. They've told me they're in desperate need of new clothing.'

Hannah's eyes glowed. 'I'd like that.'

Alex chuckled. 'I rather thought you might.'

She added cautiously, 'What about Bartholomew?'

'He's old enough to go on his own.'

'Yes, of course,' she agreed quickly, acutely aware of the sudden curtness in his voice, making her wish she hadn't mentioned the child's name.

'Now, come and sit down. Our coffee's getting cold.'

Hannah took her place at the desk, and when he sat down next to her, his long leg accidentally brushing hers, she couldn't help but wonder how on earth she was ever going to manage her coffee without spilling it all over the papers lining the smooth surface.

'You're trembling,' he remarked softly, and when her eyes swept up to meet his own, she saw they were heavy with concern.

'I...I guess it's because I'm tired,' she answered breathlessly, and tried desperately to ignore the tingling sensation sweeping up and down her arm as he lightly caressed it with his fingers.

He nodded and moved his hand up to tuck her hair gently away from her cheek. 'That's why I insisted you have a break. Not taking holidays when they're due and saving up for cruises instead isn't always a good idea.'

'I guess not,' Hannah murmured, wondering what on earth they were talking about. All she was aware of was the heady sensation of being touched and stroked by this man. 'What are you working on?' she asked, and forced herself to concentrate on the industrial maps and blueprints at the back of the massive desk.

Alex withdrew his hand and picked up one of the blueprints. He studied it silently for several seconds, and Hannah got the distinct impression that he was deciding whether or not he should share this with her.

'I've been working on a special design for a new light aircraft,' he began slowly, and spread the sheet carefully out in front of them, smoothing back the curled edges. 'It's something I've always wanted to do.'

'Like a dream project?'

He smiled. 'Sort of.'

And she knew by the smile and the simple words that he would never settle for just a dream. He began explaining his design, and Hannah's sensitive ears heard the quiet pride in his voice. 'The major structure of the design will be made out of fibreglass of aeronautical grade.'

'Fibreglass?' Hannah queried. 'Aren't planes usually built from aluminium?'

He nodded. 'Commercial aircraft especially, but that metal is subject to a vast number of problems such as corrosion and stress fractures. My aircraft will be built from composite materials, making them virtually trouble-free and much lighter and stronger.'

'But it looks so *small*!'

Alex chuckled. 'It is, and that's the beauty of it. Not only will it meet international flight and structural standards but it will be cheaper to buy than a medium-sized family car, and provided it's hangared and well maintained will have an infinite life-span.'

Hannah was impressed. 'The man on the land could certainly use this type of plane.'

'Yes, I've had a lot of interest from the rural sector. The plane would be an effective tool for managing their vast properties from the air, checking on livestock and fences. And of course, the regional businessman would benefit too, along with flying schools and other recreational markets.'

'Would it be expensive to fuel?' she asked.

'Not at all. At a cruising speed of say, a hundred and eighty kilometres per hour, I estimate a very economical eleven kilometres per litre.' He added with a grin, 'Apart from that, it will be great fun to fly.'

And as they continued to talk about the plane, their discussions leading on to the industrial land Alex had already purchased, Hannah suggested he buy an additional ten hectares to leave room for expansion.

'That way you'll be protected in the event that the land is re-zoned, which happens on a fairly regular basis here in Queensland,' she told him.

'Good advice,' he said warmly, and when she raised her eyes to his she found him watching her with a brightness she hadn't seen before, a spark of some indefinable emotion, and her own eyes responded with an inner tension of excitement.

There was a knock on the door and Mrs Buckley came in with a lunch tray. Alex and Hannah looked at each other in surprise. They hadn't realised they had been talking for well over two hours. As they lunched on crusty bread rolls, cold meats and pickles, Alex amused her with stories of his plant in Sydney and some of the antics a few of his employees had got up to. Hannah in turn told him a few amusing anecdotes of her own. Lunch passed pleasantly, with an easy camaraderie, each responding to the other's subtle wit.

'Do you ride?' Alex surprised her by asking after Mrs Buckley had collected the tray.

'You mean ... a horse?'

'Of course!'

'State champion three years running when I was a kid.'

He grinned. 'That will do.' He glanced at his watch. 'How long will it take you to change into something suitable?'

Her heart quickened with anticipation. 'Just a few moments.'

'Good. There's something I want to show you.'

Hannah felt she had wings on her feet as she floated from the study and out to the hall. At the bottom of the stairs was Mrs Buckley, with her arms loaded with fresh laundry for the children. Hannah offered to take it up for her, and Mrs Buckley handed it over with a grateful smile. As she turned to go back to her duties in the kitchen Hannah caught the worried look in her eyes.

'Is something wrong, Mrs Buckley?' she asked caringly.

The housekeeper sighed. 'It's my husband. He has an ulcer and was feeling poorly when he went off to work this morning. I keep waiting for the phone to ring, his boss telling me he's been rushed off to hospital or something.'

'I'm sure Mr Drummond wouldn't mind if you went home,' Hannah told her sympathetically.

'Yes, he'd let me off if I asked him, he's an understanding man. But I may as well worry here as all by myself at home. Besides, they know where to find me if there's an emergency.' Mrs Buckley sighed heavily and disappeared into the kitchen, while Hannah made her way up to the children's bedrooms.

She went into Bartholomew's first. His room was spartan, furnished with only the necessities; bed, bureau, wardrobe, a desk, chair and lamp. There was nothing to reveal his personality. No pictures or posters lined his walls, no books or magazines graced his desk. There wasn't even a stray sock or shoe. It was as if he hadn't actually moved in and didn't think he ever would. With a feeling of sadness, Hannah placed his fresh laundry on his bed and went into Josephine's room.

Hers wasn't much better. There was the same frigid sparseness, with one difference. Josephine had placed a small, pink pillow neatly on her bed. It seemed so lonely and vulnerable lying there, like a naked heart waiting to be crushed. Hannah shivered and laid out the clothes.

Annabelle's bedroom came as a shock. It was a glorious mass of colourful confusion. Brilliant posters covered the walls. Books, magazines, drawings, soiled socks and other discarded clothing lay in gleeful abandonment across the floor. The bed was unmade, and peeping beneath the pillow was last night's unfinished homework. Footsteps sounded in the hall and Alex came into the room.

'Have you ever seen such a mess?'

Hannah smiled at the exasperation in his voice. 'Never,' she agreed happily. 'Doesn't it look wonderful?'

'Not according to Mrs Buckley,' he chuckled. 'In fact, she refuses to come in here, and I can't say I blame her.' He added with a mock shudder, 'It looks positively dangerous.'

He took the clothes from Hannah, cleared some space on the bed and laid them down. The homework caught his attention, and he picked it up and frowned. 'I'll have a word with that young lady tonight!'

As they left the bedroom Hannah turned for another look. She wondered, suddenly, if the mess wasn't deliberate. Perhaps this was Annabelle's way of hiding from the shadows which seemed to plague all the children.

From somewhere in the huge homestead came the sound of a telephone ringing, followed almost immediately by Mrs Buckley's voice summoning Alex.

'I'll wait for you downstairs,' he told Hannah. 'Don't be long,' he added with a warning growl.

'I won't,' she promised, and slipped into her room to change into blue jeans, a bold blue and white striped jersey and brogues suitable for riding. As she applied a bit of lip-gloss and brushed her golden mane of hair she wondered what he wanted to show her, *share* with her. She was positively certain she could hear her heart singing, and it was a most wonderful sound.

Alex was waiting for her at the bottom of the stairs holding two wide-brimmed hats. He put one on her head and stood back to survey the results.

'A bit big,' he observed, 'but I can adjust the strap.' His hand felt rough against the tender skin of her chin and when he smiled into her eyes her breath caught in her throat and her heart took up a new ballad.

Two horses had already been saddled and were patiently standing under the shade of a sprawling fig tree next to the stables. One was a magnificent black stallion, while the other was a pretty young mare, her coat the colour of rich brown toffee. Hannah stroked the mare's nose and it nuzzled the palm of her hand.

Alex smiled as he watched her, his huge tanned hands resting lightly on the mare's reins. 'Do the children ride?' Hannah asked as he helped her to mount.

'Not yet, but I fully intend getting them started.' He swung a long leg easily over the saddle. 'I've suggested it a few times, but they've always balked at the idea.'

'Perhaps they're afraid?'

'It's partly that, I suppose.' A frown marred his handsome features. 'They seem afraid of so many things.'

Hannah silently agreed. 'A full-grown horse can be extremely intimidating,' she said. 'Maybe if you got them some ponies of their very own they might become more interested.'

'And maybe the kid who was state champion three years running can give them a few lessons, hmm?'

'Maybe she could,' Hannah returned with a smile. 'I know she'd like that very much.'

His eyes seemed to collide with hers. 'Then perhaps one day she shall!'

With that, Alex nudged the stallion and led the way across the rich green paddock on to an open trail. The trail cut through a young forest, narrowing gradually until eventually they emerged on to rolling green meadows, the tall grasses sprinkled with wild flowers. A clear, bubbling brook ran into a vast rock pool and above the pool shimmered a cascade of silvery water, the sun turning it into a blanket of rainbows as it poured down the rock face and into the frothing water below.

Alex drew on the reins and brought the stallion to a halt. Hannah came up alongside him, her eyes filled with delight. They didn't speak. They simply drank in the beauty before them, subdued by its awesome splendour. With a burst of incredulous joy Hannah realised this was what Alex had wanted her to see, had wanted her to share. And when he turned his dark head to gaze into her eyes and search her face, probing into her very thoughts, reaching into her soul and surrounding her heart, she felt like Eve in the Garden of Eden, and she trembled with a feverish excitement.

CHAPTER SEVEN

THEY led the horses down to one of the bubbling brooks and allowed them to drink from the crystal-clear water.

'Do you think it's safe for us to drink?' Hannah asked after they had secured their mounts under a clump of shade trees.

'It's probably safer than the water that comes from our taps,' Alex answered, and to prove it, knelt, cupped his hands, filled them with the icy cold water and drank thirstily. He filled them again. 'Try some.'

Hannah knelt beside him, her slim shoulder brushing against his massive one. Alex brought his cupped hands to her lips, but when she tried to drink, water went everywhere except in her mouth. He filled his hands again. 'Put your hands round mine,' he advised, and Hannah placed her small, slender hands around the ruggedness of his own. There was something wonderfully sensual drinking this way, and she was stirred by its intimacy as she felt her lips softly sucking against the curve of his palm.

'Would you like some more?' Alex asked in a husky whisper, and she knew he was being equally affected.

Hannah shyly shook her head. 'No, thank you.'

He smiled. 'Then it's my turn.'

'But you've already had some.'

His eyes held hers. 'I want more.'

Hannah shivered. She knew he expected her to do as he had done. 'I . . . I might spill it.'

'It wouldn't matter.'

She felt desperate now. 'But it would ruin your lovely shirt.'

'Water's never hurt it before,' he countered with a husky drawl, his smile stealing into her heart and weakening her limbs.

'All right,' she whispered, and her trembling hands went into the water and he guided them back to his lips. He drank the bit of water her small hands held, then ran his tongue into the crevices of her palms and between each slender finger, holding a pink tip between his teeth before moving on to the next. Hannah stiffened as she desperately tried to ward off the piercingly exquisite sensations mounting in her body. But when he drew her against him, she felt herself melting into the hardness of muscle and bone. Desire rose swiftly within her and her mouth eagerly met his. Their kiss was filled with the passion they had awakened in each other, and Hannah knew there would be no turning back.

Alex slipped her jersey over her head and her hair billowed in a golden cloud about her flushed face. She reached behind and unclasped her bra and he took it gently from her hands and laid it on the grass. His dark eyes savoured the beauty of her young breasts, silky white with satin-pink tips. Slowly, leisurely, he ran his fingers over them and the swollen tips hardened into erected peaks.

Hannah reached up and placed her hands against the sides of his face and drew his mouth down. She gasped her pleasure when he took the throbbing nipple into his mouth, his tongue stroking the pulsing nub. Her hands slipped under his polo shirt and she tugged it upwards, and she could never remember afterwards if she had undressed him entirely on her own or if he had provided some assistance! He leaned over her and she touched his hard male nipples, her delicate fingers teasing them into hardened peaks before trailing over the muscular wall of his chest and following the line of silky black hairs down to his navel, over the flatness of his stomach and down to the thrusting male hardness which would make them as one.

But Alex was in no hurry. He unbuttoned her jeans and drew them down to her hips, his mouth caressing the silky texture of the pale skin across her tummy before slowly slipping them further so that all which remained were her small pink bikini briefs, trimmed with white lace. His hands, so brown and hugely powerful, slipped under them and gently eased them down her long, slender legs to join the rest of their clothing on the sweet-smelling grass. For a moment his eyes feasted on the exquisite beauty of her nakedness, as Hannah had done earlier to him. His hot mouth lit fires in all the secret quivering parts of her body before he slowly entered her, his eyes never leaving her face. Then he plunged deeper and took her to heaven, and together they darted over the stars, skipped across the Milky Way and grasped the moon in a shuddering climax. A falling star glided them safely back to the soft green grass by the bubbling brook and left them to lie exhausted in each other's arms.

Alex propped himself up on his elbows and smiled lovingly down at Hannah's upturned face. Wisps of hair clung damply to her temples and he swept them back before whispering against her lips, 'The lengths a man must go to, to get himself a drink.'

'True,' Hannah whispered back, and gently tugged at a coil of hair which had fallen over his wide brow. 'I wasn't expecting to be so justly rewarded.'

'Your rewards have only just begun,' he murmured mysteriously, and kissed her long and luxuriously before rising and pulling her gently to her feet. Hannah immediately became self-conscious and folded her arms across her breasts while the fall of her hair hid her reddened cheeks.

Alex smiled, tucked her hair behind one pink little ear, took her hands into the hugeness of his own and said softly, 'There's no need for that, Hannah. We have no more secrets from each other. We can relax now and be ourselves.'

She knew he was right, and her shining eyes told him so. It was silly to be standing in front of him blushing like a virgin bride after their round trip to the moon. And when her eyes swept lovingly over him, she knew he wanted to make the trip again. Instead he led her through a stand of young she-oaks to a deep rock pool, surrounded by a bed of soft green moss. Rosellas, with their bright green, yellow and crimson plumage, darted and swooped between the branches of the gnarled old casuarina trees lining the pool. The golden sun danced through the branches from a cloudless blue sky, and it seemed to Hannah as she stood beside her handsome giant that they were the only two people in the world and this was their paradise.

'Can you swim?'

'Yes . . .' She looked anxiously up at him. 'But surely you don't want to swim in the pool?'

'Why not?'

Hannah shivered. 'Because it's far too cold.'

'Nonsense! You'll love it.'

'And it's probably filled with eels.' She shivered again.

'There's a few, but they won't bother us.'

'You go,' she told him. 'I'll watch you.'

'But it wouldn't be the same,' he drawled teasingly.

'Actually, I'm one of those people who only swim in heated indoor pools. Anything less and ... I have a tendency to drown.'

'I wouldn't let that happen.' He picked her up and jumped with her into the crystal-clear rock pool. Hannah rose spluttering and gasping for air from the icy depths. Alex rose with her, his teeth flashing white as he grinned, 'Isn't this great?'

'It's ... it's ...' Her body felt numb. She pushed her hair from her eyes and glared at him. 'I'll get you for this, Alex Drummond,' she promised solemnly.

He chuckled and wrapped his arms around her, treading water for them both. 'It's great once you get used to it.' He ran a hand down her hair. 'Feel your hair ... how soft it is.'

'My hair's *always* soft!'

He took her hand and made her touch her hair. Her eyes widened in amazed delight. Her hair felt so silky that she could barely feel it.

'There aren't any added minerals in the water,' Alex explained. 'It's totally natural.' He ran his hands over her supple body, and it wasn't the cold that made her shiver. 'Your skin feels as soft and as smooth as silk.'

'I've *always* had silky-smooth skin!'

'And now it's even silkier,' he murmured against the slender column of her neck. Hannah slipped her arms around his back and tried to decide if the natural spring water had improved the already perfect texture of his own skin.

'Do you like caves?' he whispered mysteriously against the quivering softness of her mouth.

'Caves?' she repeated uncomprehendingly, thinking how his eyes seemed even bluer today, framed by their long, spiky black lashes. She felt herself drifting into their depths.

'Uh-huh.' Alex kissed the corners of her mouth and she ran her hands through his thick black hair. 'Underwater caves.'

'Under...!' Hannah drew back her head and looked at him with alarm. 'Did you say *underwater caves*?'

'I did.'

'Where?'

He held her with one arm and indicated with the other. 'Just beneath that rock wall.'

She looked at him with horror. 'Surely you don't expect me...us...?' Her horror increased when she saw that he most certainly did. She tried unsuccessfully to break free of his arms. 'Oh, no, you don't, Alex. I've never been one for caves, especially *underwater* caves!'

He tightened his hold on her. 'You'll change your mind once you've seen this one. It's magic!'

'I've never liked magic—never! Now let go of me!' she shrieked.

'I'd never forgive myself if I didn't show you this. It's special.'

'I'll forgive you,' she was quick to assure him. 'In fact, it's something we need never mention again.'

'Surely you're not frightened?' queried Alex.

'Of course not.' She took a deep breath and let it out slowly. 'I'm absolutely terrified!'

'I'll help you deal with it.' He laid her trembling hand on his shoulder. 'You won't even need to swim, just hold on.'

Alex swam effortlessly to the moss-covered wall with Hannah clinging tightly to his shoulder. 'The entrance to the cave is approximately three metres under water,' he explained. 'When I count to three, take a deep breath and hold it until we're inside the cave.' He smiled encouragingly and patted her hand. It had taken the shape of a claw and showed promise of becoming a permanent fixture to his shoulder. 'Ready? One... two... three!'

Hannah took a deep breath, squeezed her eyes shut and felt herself being propelled at an astonishing speed to her underwater grave. Suddenly her head shot out of the water and her eyes flew open.

At first there was the sensation of light—great flashes of it as though sparked from some enormous diamonds. Then there was the colour. Brilliant colours...reds which weren't really red, because she had never before seen such a shade. Golds which were brighter than the element, blues no sky could boast, oranges, purples, pinks and all shades in between. And then there was the music! Tinkling, chiming, violins and harps, drums beating, horns blowing, angels singing! Alex watched her, enjoying the fleeting expressions of delight and wonder that took it in turns to dance across her expressive features and luminate her eyes.

'Well,' he drawled casually, 'do you like my magic cave?'

'Oh, Alex!' she breathed. 'It's incredible...it's fantastic...it's divine!' She turned her rapturous eyes to glow upon his. 'It's better than magic because it's *real*!'

He chuckled, pleased with her reaction. 'Look up there.' Together they tilted their heads back. There was a hole overhead letting in the sun, and from another opening water cascaded down the wall of the cave, catching the light and casting out rainbows, while the musical sounds splashed against the rocks and danced and skipped over the water in perfect orchestral harmony.

'However did you find it?' she asked, and her voice was filled with awe.

'By accident. I wanted to find out the depth of the pool and stumbled in here. At first I couldn't believe what I was seeing. I've explored many underwater caves in most parts of the world, but I've never come across anything quite so spectacular, or with such brilliant sounds.'

'It's so primitively beautiful,' Hannah agreed as she continued to look up and down and all around. 'It makes me feel . . . small.'

Alex grinned and drew her against him. 'You *are* small . . . and cold! Your lips have turned purple.' He placed his mouth on hers, effectively warming her. 'It's time to return to the real world,' he whispered huskily against her lips.

But as Hannah followed Alex through the opening and up to the surface, this time confident enough to do it on her own, she realised that nothing about this day had been real. It had all been incredibly fantastic, a day she knew she would treasure forever.

The sun felt warm on their bodies, chasing away the goosebumps and restoring the natural pink to Hannah's lips. She ran her hands lightly down her body and through her hair, delighting in the silky texture of both. Alex watched her, the smile on his lips matching the light in his eyes. Hannah peeped up at him through the golden tips of her lashes and grinned.

'Your hair could never feel as soft and silky as mine,' she said teasingly. 'It's far too wiry.'

And he drew her against his lean hardness, his hands running slowly through her hair and down the suppleness of her body. For a moment Hannah simply clung to him, savouring the heady scent of his body, nuzzling her cheek against the unyielding wall of his chest and thinking he smelt of red apples, freshly mown grass and newly harvested wheat. He was hers. He had made her his. Their bodies blended perfectly together. She seemed to have been created just for him, but she didn't see herself as a gift or a sacrifice. It was simply meant to be.

And while he caressed her, Hannah caressed him. At first they were gentle with each other, content simply to explore the marvels of each other's bodies, like precious jewels, until the tenderness gave way to a wild, fierce need and they dropped to the sweet-smelling grass, arms entwined, bodies locked together, and Hannah's cries of love stilled the birds and the bees and ran with the tune of the bubbling brook.

Alex gazed down at her face. Her eyes were half closed, her cheeks were flushed and her lips were swollen from passion. Gently he kissed her eyelids before easing off her. Hannah lay still for several seconds, eyes tightly shut now as her breathing slowly returned to normal. There was a pain in her heart and a burning in her eyes. She had cried out her love for him and she could still hear those joyous sounds in her ears.

But she had heard nothing back, and she felt deeply hurt. A raw, all-consuming hurt. Alex was running a finger lightly down her face, tracing the soft outline of her delicate profile. She lifted her hand. It felt so heavy, so weighted. His fingers brushed hers as she pushed his hand away, and there was a sudden flash of surprise in his eyes at the abruptness in her movement. She wanted to cry out to him, to say she hadn't meant it, hadn't meant to be so abrupt, but she was afraid she would start crying and he would want to know why she was so upset, and what could she possibly say? That you haven't told me you love me? I told *you*, so it's only fair that you should tell *me*! Of course she couldn't say such a thing. She couldn't *force* him to love her. She rose shakily to her feet, her head turned carefully away so he wouldn't see the tears brimming in her eyes. No one had ever warned her that love could be so darned painful.

'I'd better get dressed,' she said, and tried desperately to make her voice sound casual as though of course it was time to get dressed. What else did one do after one had been so wondrously loved?

Alex stretched out on his back with his hands tucked comfortably under his head and watched her pull on her clothes. There was a lazy, satisfied smile on his wicked face. Hannah wondered what he was thinking and if the smile meant he had been amused by her wild cries of love, the confessions from her tender heart. Or was he used to hearing such cries, accepting it as part of the ritual of love? Not *love*, Hannah corrected herself. *Lovemaking*. There was a big difference—a vast difference. She had felt the one, he had expertly performed the other. Anger rose swiftly and met the pain in her heart and magnified her hurt so that her whole body trembled and shook with the intensity of her emotions.

'Aren't you going to get dressed?' she snapped, and her eyes were overly bright and very green. 'Or do you intend lying there all day, naked, like a gift to the gods?'

Her words effectively erased the smile from his face and replaced it with a dark frown. She was glad. He rose slowly to a sitting position, and Hannah grabbed her shoes and pulled them on. 'And don't *ever* bring me here again,' she added as she tied up her laces with jerky, clumsy movements, aware of his dark blue eyes burning into her face.

'I thought you liked it here,' he stated calmly as he reached for his shirt and slung it over his broad tanned shoulder, his eyes intent upon her face, searching and probing.

'Well, I don't,' she lied in a quivering voice, refusing to meet those penetrating orbs as she dug the toe of her brogue into the soft green grass. 'The water was far too cold, for one thing, and

I think I got some in my lungs when you dragged me into that cave.' She added accusingly in a voice thick with unshed tears, 'I won't be at all surprised if I end up with pneumonia.'

'Well, if you do you can blame it on me,' Alex offered generously, almost cheerfully, and Hannah couldn't believe he could treat her potential condition so casually, so entirely without even the tiniest shred of remorse. He stood and slipped the polo shirt over his head and reached for his trousers, those glittering blue eyes never leaving her face. 'Anything else?' he asked almost purringly.

She bravely kept the tears at the backs of her eyes as she slowly drew in her breath and let it out again in a quivering sigh. 'You should have told me to bring a bathing suit.'

Had she dared to look at him she would have seen the amused tenderness dancing in his eyes and the smile that moved lazily across his face. 'Bathing suits are for indoor, heated pools.' He did up the buckle of his belt and sat down beside her. Instantly she stiffened, but was powerless to move even a short distance away. His face was turned towards her, but she stared straight ahead, seeing nothing, feeling only his closeness and wishing . . . wishing he would take her in his arms and hating herself for her weakness. 'Besides, I didn't know I'd be showing you my cave . . . at least, not today.'

Her head spun around. 'That's a lie, Alex Drummond, a deliberate *lie*! You said you wanted to *show* me something.'

'I did.' He waved an expansive arm, taking in the babbling brooks, the moss-circled rock pools, the glistening, silvery waterfalls, the flower-dotted meadows and the tall stately trees hosting the colourful birds beneath the brilliant blue sky. '*This*!' He stretched out on the grass, supporting himself on one elbow. 'The property's on the market. I'm negotiating to buy it.'

Hannah stared at him. 'You mean...it doesn't already belong to you? We...we're *trespassing*?'

Alex chuckled. 'I guess a solicitor might use that term, but I prefer to think of us as simply *visiting*.'

Hannah jumped to her feet. The tears she had been desperately holding back finally betrayed her, filled her eyes and rolled down her cheeks. Alex immediately sat up, his eyes darkened with concern, and reached for her hand, but Hannah backed away, angrily swiping at those wretched tears. He had made love to her on someone else's land—land he was considering buying when he already owned so much. But that wasn't the point. The point was he would need a solicitor to do the conveyancing! This morning she had been especially proud of showing off her legal expertise, had thrilled in the knowledge of their ability to work together, their two worlds merging

into what she considered a perfect partnership.
Obviously he had thought so too and intended
to *use* her! Her mind whirled crazily, wondering
how he would do that. Of course! He probably
thought she would do his legal work for *nothing*!
My God! she thought. There was no romance in-
volved here; that had never been his intention.
He had simply mixed business with pleasure.
What a fool she had been to think he had planned
something special just for her, for *them*. And how
willingly, how easily she had been led into his
trap. How he must have smiled to himself when
she had cried out her love for him. It must have
seemed like dollars in the bank! This last dreadful
thought filled her with a burning defiance and
effectively dried her tears. Her eyes turned cold
and wary and she wished she could hate him, but
how could she when even now just looking at
him was enough to send her poor ignorant heart
skipping crazily across her chest. He smiled his
slow wonderful smile and leaned forward to take
her cold little hand into the magnificent warmth
of his and she knew he had the ability to charm
the skin off a snake. And for this there was no
antidote.

'Sit down, Hannah,' he purred softly, and as
she felt herself slowly but firmly being pulled
down she glanced at the horses grazing nearby
and knew the sensible thing to do would be to
pull her hand free and ride like blazes away from

this man and his Garden of Eden. That would be the smart thing, but instead of tugging her hand free she actually found her fingers tightening around his own and soon she was sitting next to the handsome rogue under the tree. I'm weak, she thought, and compensated for this inadequacy by making sure she didn't sit too close to him, that not even a thread of their clothing touched. She needn't have bothered. Alex simply moved closer to her, his hard thigh pressed against hers, their shoulders nudging. I could always move, she thought, but I can't because of this sudden terrible weakness I've developed. And so Hannah gave in to it and listened to the warm deep timbre of his voice.

'I've been negotiating for months now,' Alex told her, and added forcefully, 'And I mean to get it.'

'Because of the cave?' Hannah asked quietly, and her eyes drifted to the moss-covered wall, the churning water beneath and the hidden splendour of the treasure it guarded.

'Not only the cave. There's a small rain forest just over that hill, and beyond that lies a cluster of freshwater lakes. The soil is rich and fertile, and water would never be a problem.'

'So you intend to farm it?' She felt oddly disappointed. 'Cut down all the trees, plough up the meadows? And sell the timber in the rain

forest too, I suppose,' she added on a sad note
of despair.

'Certainly *not*!' he declared with such ve-
hemence that Hannah jumped. 'How could you
suggest such a thing?'

She frowned, puzzled, then her expression
became wary. 'You're going to *develop* it?' She
made the word sound sinful.

'Of course not!'

'Then what *are* you going to do with it?'

Alex studied her for several long seconds, seconds in which Hannah felt him dipping into her
soul. 'What would you do with it?' he asked her
softly.

'Me?' Her lovely eyes drifted across the fresh
green meadows, the bubbling rock pools, the wild
flowers dancing in the soft breezes, the sun-kissed
trees, and she breathed deeply of the pure, sweet
air.

And thought of the concrete jungle surrounded by barbed wire fencing which served to
reform delinquent teenagers. And the hundreds
of street kids without homes to call their own,
most of whom had forgotten what it was like to
sit at a table and eat a decent meal or to sleep in
a bed. And she knew exactly what she would do
if she had a property such as this and the re-
sources with which to carry it out.

'I'd build little white bungalows,' she began
dreamily. 'Each would have a different coloured

roof. They would have three bedrooms, bright kitchens, big lounge-rooms, a bathroom and a laundry. Each bungalow would have its own garden and fruit trees.' She sighed deeply and looked at Alex. 'That's what I'd do with a property like this.'

'Little white bungalows with different coloured roofs?'

Hannah nodded, and sighed again. 'Each with its own garden.' Her eyes drifted wistfully across the lush green meadows.

'And may I be so bold as to enquire what you'd do with these little dwellings?'

'I'd fill them with house parents and children.'

'You'd do *what*?' He grabbed both her hands and stared at her with a dawning horror. 'What sort of children? Not... *delinquents*?'

She nodded and the dreamy expression slowly faded from her eyes. 'It's just a dream I sometimes have,' she said simply. 'I don't expect it to come true.'

'I should hope not!' Alex sprang to his feet, his face dark. 'Even the thought of hundreds of kids, delinquent ones at that, tearing through this magnificent place, destroying everything in sight... good grief, Hannah, I've never heard of such a crazy idea!' He glared down at her. 'I'm going to put it from my mind, and I suggest you do the same.'

'I already have.'

'Good.' He sighed his relief and sat back down beside her. Together they stared across the meadows. 'How old would these kids be?' he asked with a growl.

'Anywhere between six and seventeen.'

'*Six*? Good heavens!'

'That's the youngest I've seen.' Hannah picked a blade of grass and put it in her mouth.

'But what about foster-homes? What about their *own* homes?'

'Foster-homes are hard to find, and they prefer the streets to what's offered them in their own homes.'

'Maybe they're just too fussy.'

Hannah turned slowly to face him. There was a deep sadness in her eyes. 'Children don't like being abused. They hate the constant beatings, the physical, sexual and mental abuse. They don't take kindly to a different father or mother every week who's always drunk or crazy with drugs.' She sighed heavily. 'They're not fussy, Alex, they simply want to survive.'

'It's not our problem,' he answered curtly.

'I wonder whose problem it is?' Hannah asked innocently as she picked another blade of grass and sucked on the juicy end. 'Everyone says it isn't theirs, but it must belong to *someone*!'

'It does. Charitable organisations. I give handsomely several times a year.'

'Sometimes...that's not enough.' She drew up her knees and hugged them against her chest. 'So what do you propose to do with this property?' There was a barely perceptible catch in her voice.

'Nothing! I want to preserve it, leave it as it is, in its natural state.'

Hannah nodded. 'Your own private paradise.'

'Exactly!'

'To be enjoyed exclusively by yourself.'

'If you're trying to make me feel guilty I can tell you right now you're not succeeding.'

'Guilty?' She glanced at him in surprise. 'I wasn't thinking any such thing.'

Suddenly he laughed—great, huge booming sounds which roared across the peaceful meadows and startled the wildlife.

'What's so funny?' Hannah asked, astonished.

'You!' He roared again. 'You really had me going for a minute! Little white bungalows with different coloured roofs filled with Artful Dodgers on a three-and-a-half-million-dollar parcel of land!' He wiped the corners of his eyes and shook his dark head. 'You know, it never fails to amaze me how some people with usually no money of their own can come up with the darnedest, most virtuous ways to spend other people's hard-earned cash!'

Hannah's face flamed and her eyes clouded with an angry hurt. 'You asked me what I'd do and I told you.'

She jumped to her feet, and the tears which had been threatening her for so long sprang to her eyes and formed tiny silvery droplets on her long, curling lashes before rolling down her cheeks. 'I told you my *dream*!' she whispered brokenly. 'I didn't...I never expected you to *laugh*!'

And she turned and ran blindly towards the pretty little mare.

CHAPTER EIGHT

ALEX caught her as she was about to mount the
mare.

'Let go of me!' Hannah screeched as she tried
to wrench her arm free, but Alex merely
strengthened his grip.

'You're not riding in this condition,' he told
her tightly. 'Either calm down or walk back to
the homestead.'

'Walk?' she spluttered. 'Walk, you say?' She
could hardly believe her ears. 'It must be at least
eight kilometres.'

'Ten, to be exact.' He released her and she
stood there, looking straight at him, tears rolling
down her flushed cheeks. Alex sighed deeply,
reached into his pocket and pulled out a snowy
white, man-sized handkerchief. He dabbed gently
at her cheeks while fresh tears splashed on to his
hand. Hannah grabbed the handkerchief, his
gentleness too much for her, and rubbed viciously
at her eyes and face, blew her nose rather loudly
and stuffed it into her own pocket.

'I'm calm now,' she sniffed in a wavering voice.
She took the reins and started to mount, but
somehow couldn't manage to get her foot into

the stirrup. Huge hands circled her waist and she felt herself being lifted on to the stallion. Alex took the mare's reins, sprang easily on to the saddle in front of her, and there was nothing for Hannah to do but wrap her arms about his waist, press her cheek against his back and endure the humiliation of having to ride double all the way back to the homestead . . . she who had been state champion three years running!

Within half an hour of arriving, Hannah was ready to leave. Alex met her at the bottom of the stairs. His eyes swept from her face to the suitcase she was carrying, and he nodded.

'Yes, I thought you might do this.'

'And please don't try to stop me.' Her voice sounded shaky, but her chin was set in a stubborn line. She swept past him, dragging her suitcase after her.

'What do you want me to tell Josephine and Annabelle?' his voice drawled behind her. 'After all, you did promise to take them shopping.'

Hannah turned slowly to face him. It was clear by her expression that she had forgotten all about the proposed shopping expedition. 'I didn't promise them,' she said guiltily. 'You asked me and I . . . I . . .'

'Promised you would,' he finished for her.

'And you've already told them?'

'I have, this morning at breakfast. You can't imagine how excited they were.' He was lounging against the wall, feet crossed at the ankles. 'They'll be home from school any minute now.' He lifted a huge hand and examined his finger-nails. 'What should I tell them?'

'Well, for a start you shouldn't have promised them anything until after you'd checked with me,' Hannah told him.

'So you want me to say you don't want to take them shopping?' He sighed deeply. 'They'll be so upset!'

Hannah shrugged her shoulders helplessly. Alex had her and he knew it. She wouldn't let the children down. Her hand tightened on the handle of the suitcase. But she couldn't stay here. Not now. Not after they had made love and Alex knew exactly how she felt about him. Not after he had scoffed at her dream.

'Tell the girls...' She cleared her throat. 'Tell the girls I had to leave, but I'll be around to-morrow morning...around ten...and we'll go shopping then.'

Alex shook his head. 'Saturdays are out. Annabelle has dancing and Josephine likes to go to the library.'

Hannah felt trapped. 'So it has to be today?'

He nodded. 'Straight after school.' He reached out for her suitcase and took it from her limp fingers.

'Is there anything else you've told the children I should know about?' she asked stiffly.

He frowned as he thought. 'Nothing comes to mind.'

'Thank goodness.' She glanced at her suitcase. 'Maybe I could leave that here in the hall and pick it up after I've returned the girls?'

Alex snapped his fingers. 'That reminds me—there *is* something I forgot to mention.'

Hannah's eyes narrowed suspiciously. 'What is it?'

'Do you remember that telephone call I took just before we went on our ride?'

'Yes,' she answered slowly, eyes still narrowed.

'Well, it was concerning Mr Buckley. He's quite ill.'

Concern replaced the suspicion in Hannah's eyes. 'He hasn't been taken to hospital, has he?'

'No, but he's got to take some time off work and he needs Mrs Buckley to take care of him. Naturally, I told her to go…to take as much time as she needs. She was worried about the children, but I assured her you'd be here for the next few days, so she went off quite happily.'

Hannah stared at him. She was certain she saw a flash of triumph burn brightly in his eyes. 'For the next few days?' she repeated weakly.

'Uh-huh. Of course, I realise I should have checked with you first, but how was I to know you'd suddenly change your mind about staying?' he drawled with all the innocence of a newborn lamb.

A deep flush lapped quickly across her face. She couldn't possibly stay under the same roof as this man, not for a few days, not even for one day. She loved him too much to have her heart trampled on, the pieces broken and tossed away, as she felt certain would surely happen. If only she hadn't told him how she felt then maybe, just maybe, she might have been able to brazen her way through a few days of seeing him, listening to his voice, waiting for the smile which could melt her heart, knowing his bedroom was not far from hers. She chewed on her bottom lip, not daring to look at him, when suddenly, mercifully she thought of Mimi. She felt faint with relief and her eyes swept up to meet Alex's. He had been quietly watching her.

'I have the perfect solution,' she said with a rush. 'Mimi! She loves children and children love her. Mimi would be perfect.'

Alex frowned. 'Mimi? Sounds like a poodle.'

Hannah grinned. 'She's my housekeeper and she's already met Bartholomew. Of course, I'd need to check with her first, but I'm almost positive she'll agree to come here for a few days or until Mrs Buckley returns. She has no family ties and——'

'Not a chance!' Alex tossed away the eager suggestion with a dismissive wave of his hand. 'I haven't the desire nor the time to break in another housekeeper, especially one who'll only be needed for such a short while.' He impaled her with his eyes. 'You said you'd stay and I'm holding you to your word.' He added meaningfully, 'Unless, of course, all that talk about caring for kids was just that—*talk*!'

Hannah's colour rose to new heights. She knew, finally, that there was no backing out. The kitchen door slammed at the back of the house, announcing the children's arrival home from school. Annabelle's voice roared, 'Hannah! Miss Baker? Where are you? Are we going shopping now or what?'

Alex's black brows rose questioningly. 'Well, Hannah,' he asked softly, 'what do you intend to do?'

What could she do? It would have seemed churlish and irresponsible to refuse. Annabelle roared again. Hannah looked helplessly in the direction of the kitchen and then up at the dark censure in Alex's eyes. 'I'll stay,' she whispered, and her heart thumped in her chest as though it too had been waiting for her reply.

Alex let his breath out slowly. Hannah knew it was from relief. She would have loved to have thought it was because he wanted her with him, just as she longed for his company, but of course she knew better. He was a busy man. He needed someone to keep an eye on the children. Nevertheless she lost herself in the slow smile that edged itself across his face. 'That's my girl!' he drawled. Hannah watched him make his way up the stairs, humming softly. '*My girl*'! he had called her. If only it were true, she thought with a despondent sigh as she turned and hurried towards the kitchen to greet her three charges.

'Should we change out of our school uniforms?' Josephine wanted to know after the initial greetings were over and Hannah had explained Mrs Buckley's absence.

'Nah, that would waste time,' Annabelle answered before Hannah had a chance to open her mouth. 'We've got our own credit cards. Let's just get going.'

Hannah looked at Bartholomew. He had opened a carton of milk and a packet of chocolate-chip cookies and was sitting at the kitchen table. He had turned his back on Hannah and hadn't responded to her greeting.

'Why don't you join us, Bartholomew?' she asked gently, thinking he might be feeling left out.

'I shop by myself,' he told her curtly. He picked up the milk and drank straight from the carton, leaving cookie crumbs on the edge. 'That way I can shoplift in peace!'

'Oh, Bartholomew,' Josephine sighed. 'Why must you say such things to Hannah?'

'Yes,' Annabelle agreed, and punched him lightly on his shoulder. 'Especially as she had her house broken into and stuff stolen.'

'I'm surprised she hasn't accused me of taking them,' he drawled, and took another long gulp of milk, swallowing noisily, which Hannah knew was done deliberately. The noise didn't disturb her, but not using a glass certainly did. She realised the combination of the two plus the remark about shoplifting was meant to goad, so she wisely let it pass.

But Bartholomew wasn't about to let her off so easily. 'So you're our new maid,' he said sneeringly, eyeing her up and down. 'You're certainly prettier than Mrs Buckley, but I wonder if you're as fast.' He picked up the carton of milk and spilt the contents on to the floor. 'Let's see how long it takes you to clean it up.'

Josephine gasped and covered her mouth with her hands. Annabelle giggled nervously. Bartholomew dumped the remainder of the chocolate chip cookies on to the floor and ground them into the milk with the heel of his shoe.

'There,' he crowed, 'that should make your job a little more interesting.'

The three children watched her, each with a different expression, wondering what she would do. Josephine was white with shock. Annabelle was clearly expecting a battle royal. Bartholomew was triumphantly challenging.

Hannah gazed thoughtfully down at the gooey mess trickling its way across the floor. 'It certainly is interesting,' she agreed slowly. 'I've seen the same sort of work at art galleries,' she confided seriously, her golden eyes focused on Bartholomew's disbelieving blue ones. 'Of course, there the art is displayed on canvases, but the floor works. It's certainly big enough . . . and smooth . . . plenty of room for scope.' They heard Alex's footsteps coming down the hall. Hannah took a last admiring glance at Bartholomew's masterpiece before taking the girls' hands and leading them towards the door. 'Let's hope your uncle appreciates art as much as I do,' she told him kindly, but as they made their way towards her car Alex's disbelieving roar told them he was no connoisseur of domestic doodlings!

Shopping was fun . . . and exhausting. Annabelle loved anything and everything, especially if it appeared in all the colours of a fluorescent rainbow. Josephine was the opposite, almost painfully conservative. Her prized purchases were three small white bras which Annabelle insisted her sister definitely didn't need. Hannah treated them to milkshakes in a bright little café before they headed back to the homestead. The girls immediately dashed up to their bedrooms to try on their new outfits. Hannah found a note on the kitchen table with her name scrawled across it in bold black print.

Her hands trembled as she picked it up. It seemed to come alive as she held it. She knew it was from Alex—she recognised his handwriting.

Her heart fluttered in her chest. She unfolded it carefully, smiling at the words.

> Trust the shopping went well. I'll be up around seven for dinner. Hope you're a good cook! Alex.

Hannah read the brief note several times, and to her it was as good as a love letter. She loved the bold scrawl of his hand, and never before had her name been written in such a way. She folded it carefully and tucked it into her pocket.

Humming happily, she removed a leg of lamb from the well stocked freezer, topped it with mint and put it in the oven. The girls came downstairs, each proudly sporting a new outfit which Hannah duly admired. Annabelle was dressed in a bright yellow frock with slashes of a brilliant orange woven through the fabric. With her dark colouring it certainly looked attractive. She would have preferred seeing the child without the stilettos, but knew Annabelle loved them and so said nothing. Josephine had pinned her hair up and she looked like an elegant, delicate flower in a rose-coloured jumper and matching trousers with little white sandals on her slender feet. They surprised Hannah by asking if there was anything they could do to help.

'I'd like you to set the dining table in the family room,' Hannah instructed them. 'I'm preparing a special meal fit for a king.' She added with an impish grin, 'And for the king's nieces and nephew, of course.'

Their answering grins told her they liked this idea, and, to prove it, they got out the best table-cloth, crockery and cutlery which they said was reserved for very special occasions. While the girls fussed over their chore Hannah slipped outside to pick fresh flowers for their centrepiece. As she followed the tiled path outside Alex's den a sudden movement caught her attention, and through the opened french doors she saw Bartholomew. He was standing in front of the huge family portrait hanging above the mantel. His body was rigid, his head bowed, and it seemed to Hannah he was doing...*a penance*!

She watched him, not daring to breathe. He stood in this painfully awkward position for several moments before finally lifting his head, and as he did so he saw Hannah. Neither moved. Anger flared in his eyes, but not before she had witnessed the cloak of grief which had dulled them. She stood there, arms filled with the flowers she had picked, and her eyes reflected the pain she knew he carried in his heart.

'Bartholomew,' she said, her voice barely above a whisper as she stepped inside the room. He backed away, his face flushed now with rage.

'You were *spying* on me!' The words were choked.

Hannah shook her head. 'No...no, I wasn't,' she responded quietly. 'I——'

'Yes, you *were*!' He ran towards the door and flung it open. 'But you didn't see *nothing*!' The door slammed behind him as he ran into the hall.

Hannah walked over to the mantel. The chill she had experienced earlier swept over her as she lifted her face to the painting. She stepped closer. The chill grew more intense.

She wondered now how she had ever thought it beautiful. It was ugly in its stiffness, stark in its frigidness, cruel in its coldness. There were no smiles on their lips, no loving lights in their eyes. But there was something more, something which was constantly evading her. Hannah stepped closer still. Suddenly her mind was flooded with photographs from her own family albums. Mentally she skipped through them—and with a jolt it came to her. Nobody in the picture above the mantel was *touching* each other! It was as though something had happened to pull them apart. Shaken, Hannah left the study. She heard the roar of Bartholomew's trail bike, followed by the frantic shouts of Josephine and Annabelle as they screamed for him to come back. Hannah hurried towards them and, sobbing hysterically, they told her Bartholomew had gone and that he was never coming back!

Hannah calmed them as best she could before picking up the house phone to ring down to the Garden Centre and speak to Alex.

'Don't worry,' he reassured her, 'I think I know where he might be. Tell the girls I'll have their brother back in time for dinner.'

Relieved, Hannah repeated the message to the distraught children. And then the wait began. The oven was turned down, the girls fussed over the table, straightening napkins and rearranging the flowers Hannah had picked. Hannah watched them with pity in her eyes. Their pale little faces were drawn and pinched. They were more worried than any child should ever be. The table gave them something to focus on, and Hannah knew they wanted everything to be just perfect for their brother when their uncle Alex returned him home. She turned the oven lower. Two hours passed before they heard the Range Rover pull up to the house. The girls ran to hug their brother, but Bartholomew pushed them aside. He was soaking wet and covered with dirt. Alex sent him upstairs to shower and dress for dinner, then turned to Hannah and asked her to join him in the study. She saw the strain around his eyes and his complexion was ashen.

'Sit down,' he told her when they were safely inside the study. She remained silent as she watched him pace the floor, and her heart ached for him. When he spoke, his voice was filled with a raw emotion. 'I found him on that block of land I showed you. He didn't see me. He was sitting beneath a tree . . . writing.' Alex dragged a weary hand roughly through his hair. 'After a while he got up, found a rock and put it over the papers he'd been writing on. He started to walk along the brook. There was a wind and despite the rock the papers began to scatter. He was out of sight by then, so I picked them up. I . . .' He stared at Hannah, his eyes filled with anguish and when he spoke again his voice was hoarse. 'I saw it was a letter—to his parents! He begged their forgiveness for killing them!'

Colour drained from Hannah's face and her hand flew to her mouth. '*No*!' she gasped.

Alex ran a shaken hand across his jaw. 'Nothing he'd written made any sense. He wasn't anywhere near his parents when they died, but over and over he begged for their forgiveness. I heard a splash, and I ran after him. He was in the water. I dragged him out . . .' His eyes held Hannah's across the room. She knew he was silently telling her what she had already feared. Bartholomew had tried killing himself. 'I shook him,' he continued in a low voice. 'He kicked and yelled, and still I shook him. And then I grabbed him and held him in my arms. He started to cry. It was horrendous. I've never heard anyone cry like that, and God! I never want to again.' A long shuddering sound escaped from

Alex's lips, and Hannah jumped up from her chair and flew over to him. She touched the grieving lines in his face and pulled his head down to kiss him fully on the mouth. His arms swept around her and they clung to each other, and as she listened to the pounding of his heart against her cheek she knew he was listening to the torturous sounds of a little boy crying. He might not love me, she thought as tears burned in her own eyes, but he needs me, and that's good enough.

A hesitant knock sounded on the door, followed by a plaintive voice. 'Uncle Alex...Hannah...can't we eat now?'

Only Hannah knew the pain in Alex's heart as he pushed it aside to comment on the girls' new outfits and to say how pretty they looked. He admired the artistry of the table, adding to the children's delight, and all the while Hannah knew he was listening for the sound of Bartholomew's footsteps coming down the stairs to join them for dinner.

The vegetables were set on the table alongside the roast. Alex pulled out a chair for Hannah and did the same for the girls. Annabelle giggled, but Josephine looked anxious. 'Aren't we going to wait for Bartholomew?' she asked.

'He'll be down in a moment,' Alex told her. 'He just needs a bit of time to himself.' He took his own place at the table and picked up the

carving knife. 'By the time I've carved this I'm
sure he'll be down.'

Thick slices of meat were put on each of their
plates, and Hannah added generous portions of
creamy whipped potatoes, fresh green beans and
tender baby carrots. The gravy was passed
around, grace was said, but still Bartholomew
hadn't made an appearance.

Suddenly Alex stiffened, and Hannah followed his glance to the rustic stone arch.
Bartholomew stood there, hands and face still
covered with grime and wearing the same muddy
wet clothes. His face was swollen from his earlier
crying and a red rage burned in his eyes. That
rage was focused entirely on Hannah.

'I thought you'd gone!' he screamed. His head
whipped around to Alex. 'Make her *leave*! We
don't *want* her here!' He ran sobbing towards
the table and knocked the remainder of the roast
on to the floor. Alex stood up from his chair and
grabbed him firmly by the arm.

'That will be enough, Bartholomew,' he said
firmly in a deadly calm voice.

Bartholomew struggled to free himself from
the iron-hard grip while he screamed out abuse
at Hannah. Josephine and Annabelle looked on
in a stunned silence, and Hannah's heart went
out to them. Their little faces were an unnatural
white, their eyes blackened holes of horror. Their

knives and forks were poised over their plates, suspended in time.

'I hate you!' Bartholomew sobbed, his voice hoarse. His eyes flew wildly around the table, stabbing each in turn. 'I hate all of you!' Alex released him and he tore from the room.

Josephine rose slowly from her chair. Her body was rigid. She could have been a robot. And when she spoke, her voice sounded mechanical, as if it had come from some bloodless thing.

'May I be excused, Uncle Alex?'

At first Hannah thought he might refuse her request, but his eyes only deepened with despair at the sight of her frozen little face. 'Yes, go ahead,' he answered quietly.

Josephine marched stiffly from the family room, through to the kitchen, down the hall and up the stairs. Her feet made small shuffling sounds like those of an old woman. Hannah squeezed her eyes shut, and tears glistened on her lashes.

'May I go too?' Annabelle's husky little voice shivered across the painful silence. 'They'll need me.' She looked pleadingly at her uncle Alex. A sad smile touched his mouth as he nodded. Annabelle glanced down at the meal she hadn't touched and slipped down from her chair.

Neither Hannah nor Alex spoke as they listened to Annabelle's stilettos clatter their lonely journey up to join her brother and sister. Upstairs a door slammed. It seemed to echo repeatedly around their ears. Then Hannah and Alex were wrapped in a most dreadful silence.

And in that dreadful silence Hannah knew what she must do. She must leave, now, never to return. The tortured forces at work in Bartholomew's mind were using her to speed him along his path of self-destruction—a path which would eventually destroy this little family.

She thought of the enormous amount of work Alex had done to provide a happy, cheerful environment for his little brood, and she remembered Josephine's desperate plea: 'Everything's just starting to get nice. Please don't spoil it'.

As if reading her mind, Alex reached across the table and took her cold, trembling hands into his. The anguish in his eyes matched her own. With enormous difficulty Hannah managed to drag her eyes from the face she loved and stared blindly through her tears down at their hands so tightly entwined.

'I can't let you go,' he whispered hoarsely. And then the words she had waited so long to hear. 'I love you, Hannah! I love you too much to lose you now.'

Tears glistened across the heartbreak in her eyes. 'What can we do?' she whispered brokenly.

His hands tightened around hers. 'I'll think of something. We must be patient, my darling.'

CHAPTER NINE

HANNAH stood at the top of the stairs of the court-house building. She was smartly dressed in a black and white checked suit with a rust-coloured roll-necked top beneath the tailored jacket. In her hand was her briefcase. The wind picked up her honey-blonde hair and tossed it gently about her face. Unconsciously she brushed it aside, while her golden eyes searched the scurrying crowds on the pavement below. She was waiting for Alex.

Then she saw him, and the anxiety flew from her eyes and was replaced with a tender yearning. His dark head and broad shoulders rose above the milling crowd as he swiftly made his way to the court-house. He was dressed in a dark blue suit, pale blue shirt and a maroon tie. Hannah was struck as she always was by his devastating good lucks, and actually sympathised with the female eyes that followed him down the street.

He saw her at the top of the stairs, and for a moment their eyes met and each saw the other's anguish before the brilliant light of their love broke through the grey cloud of their mutual despair. Hannah ran down to meet him, and he grasped her hands and held tightly on to them while his eyes searched her lovely face. 'Are you all right?' he asked earnestly.

'Yes,' she answered softly, 'I'm fine.' Her eyes searched his face, her expression once again anxious. 'And you?'

He smiled down at her. 'Now that I'm with you, great!' He tucked her briefcase under his arm and she matched his step to the little side-street restaurant which had become their meeting place over the past two months. It was smart, elegant, and their privacy was ensured. The *maître d'hôtel* led them immediately to their table, which Alex always had in reserve.

Time was too precious to spend mulling over the menu selection. Each ordered the same, usually a seafood salad and a crisp white wine. They only had an hour, the time of Bartholomew's appointment with the child psychologist.

'Do you think he'll open up to the doctor this time?' Hannah asked with a quiet hope.

Alex shook his head. 'I doubt it. He seems to be sinking deeper and deeper within himself. They've suspended him from school. He rarely talks, refuses to eat with us, spends his days sitting in his room or staring at the television.' He dragged a hand roughly through his thick black hair and added with a worried frown, 'The house seems like a morgue. It's having a dreadful effect on the girls.'

'How's Mimi coping?'

'Wonderfully well. I don't know what the girls would do without her.' He reached into his pocket and withdrew a small pink envelope. 'Before I forget, here's a note from Josephine.' He smiled as he passed it to her. 'She made me swear on a stack of bibles that I wouldn't forget to give it to you!'

Hannah opened the envelope and carefully removed the single pink sheet.

Dear Hannah, I pray each night that soon you'll come and visit us and that B.'s doctor will make him better. A. sends her love, as do I. Yours most sincerely, Josephine Drummond.

Hannah read the note several times while tears welled in her eyes and rolled down her cheeks. Her hands trembled as she put the pink sheet back into its envelope.

'Oh, Alex,' she whispered as the sobs she was holding in check racked her insides, 'what are we going to do?'

He took her frozen hands into the firm, reassuring warmth of his own. 'We're going to hold on as we've been doing,' he said quietly, his eyes darkened at the sight of the tears glistening on the pale beauty of her heart-shaped face. He raised her hands to his mouth and gently kissed each fingertip, their eyes tortured as they silently gazed at each other.

'The next two days will be ours,' he whispered hoarsely. 'Are you looking forward to it?'

Butterflies chased away the blues and danced in her stomach. A warm flush spread across her smooth cheeks.

'You know I am,' she answered, and he smiled at the sudden shyness in her voice and kissed the moist warmth of her palm. 'I'm all packed.'

In fact, ever since Alex had invited her to accompany him on a two-day business trip to Sydney to hold meetings on the design of his new plane Hannah had been barely able to think of anything else. Two whole precious days to spend with the man she loved, the man she adored.

'Are you sure the children will be all right?' she asked anxiously. 'Josephine and Annabelle are one hundred per cent over their flu?'

'One hundred per cent,' he assured her solemnly, while the corners of his mouth lifted in a smile. 'Just make sure you don't get sick on me. If anything happens to our two days...' His voice trailed off while a deep, dark passion filled the liquid depths of his smouldering blue eyes. 'I've arranged for the penthouse suite,' he continued huskily. 'I want everything to be perfect.'

A sudden, unexplained tension gripped her and spread uneasily into her eyes. She grasped tightly on to his hands. 'Do you feel guilty?' she asked.

'Not at all.' He frowned, watching her closely. 'And neither should you.' He pulled her towards him and kissed her passionately. 'I love you, darling,' he whispered against her lips. 'I love you and I need you.'

Hannah's eyes closed as she kissed him back. 'I know,' she husked, and thought of how once she had worried that he mightn't. How foolish she had been then, and how trivial her little worries now seemed. 'Do you think we'll have time for business?'

He smiled devilishly. 'Probably not!'

She ran her tongue teasingly across his lips. 'Your solicitor will make certain we keep to schedule.'

He chuckled softly. 'Not if she does what she's doing now, she won't.'

Hannah lifted her hand and lovingly traced the strong line of his jaw. 'I won't be able to sleep tonight thinking about tomorrow. And then I'll look ghastly with bags under my eyes.'

'I have a good remedy for bags.' He framed her heart-shaped face with his huge tanned hands and gently kissed her eyelids. 'So don't worry about looking anything less than beautiful,' he growled.

'I won't,' she promised softly, and closed her eyes again. Alex smiled and pressed his mouth against her eyelids because he knew this was what she wanted. The love in his eyes burned with a fierce intensity, while a tiny nerve throbbed alongside his jaw. Nothing will go wrong tomorrow, my darling, he promised her silently. *Nothing!*

Hannah was dressed and waiting for Alex at seven o'clock the following morning. She was wearing beige linen trousers, topped with a dark green pullover. Her hair fell loosely to her shoulders in a glorious shining curve. Her bag was packed and so was her briefcase.

Apart from the plane's design, Alex would also sign the last remaining documents for the purchase of the block of land he had shown her and which they had affectionately named Paradise. He had steadfastly refused to tell her what he planned doing with it, and Hannah suspected he would tell her during the next two days. Her only concern was that he might build a tourist resort, which was precisely what the other contenders for the beautiful property had intended.

The Mercedes sports convertible pulled up at her front steps and Alex leaped out. He was dressed as casually as Hannah in cream trousers and a black long-sleeved sweater, the sleeves pushed back on his deeply tanned forearms. Hannah opened the door and flew into his arms. He smelt heavenly and felt just as great.

'All set?' he murmured against her cheek.

'All set,' she answered happily, basking in his nearness and his warmth.

He set her bag and her briefcase into the Mercedes and helped her into the vehicle. 'Mimi has the telephone number of our hotel in Sydney?' she asked as he started the powerful motor.

Alex chuckled and gave her thigh a squeeze. 'You know she does. Now stop worrying. Our Mimi's an extremely capable person. Nothing will happen during the next two days that she won't be able to handle.' He added seriously with an enigmatic gleam in the electric-blue of his eyes, 'Our two days have started. They're ours to enjoy!'

But the closer they got to the airport the more the feeling of foreboding Hannah had experienced the previous day intensified. It was ridiculous, she knew, but she couldn't fight the uneasy notion that Bartholomew was watching them. When Alex drove past the domestic terminal to the private one and parked close to a smart, gleaming white four-seater plane she felt gripped with an almost suffocating panic.

'I . . . I can't fly in *that*! she choked. 'It . . . it's too *small*!'

She went on to explain this ridiculous phobia she had about flying, and while Alex listened sympathetically she still found herself strapped in a seat next to him in the cockpit. She stared at him with horror.

'You're the *pilot?*!'

Alex chuckled. 'Oh, ye of little faith.'

Hannah squeezed her eyes shut on take-off and landing, but apart from that she realised she had been less nervous than on any commercial flights she had taken. And watching his capable hands on the controls and listening to the quiet authority in his deep voice as he spoke to the air traffic controllers had only heightened her respect and admiration for the man.

The hotel he had booked them into was a picture of romantic elegance facing Sydney's famous Harbour.

'This is absolutely beautiful, Alex,' Hannah told him with glowing eyes. The spacious three-roomed suite was decorated with olde-worlde charm. There were connecting bedrooms, each with its own high wide four-poster bed with silk canopies and private *en-suites*. Carved wardrobes stood majestically against the walls and there were soft blue velvet love-seats nestled in corners and ornate writing desks beneath gold-framed landscapes of Old Sydney Town. French doors opened on to private balconies shaded by stately Alexandra palms towering from the lush green gardens below. Hannah stepped on to the balcony leading from the spacious lounge-room, and Alex followed her.

Beyond lay a panoramic view of pink sandstone cliffs overhanging the sparkling blue waters of the sweeping Sydney Harbour. Hydrofoils, catamarans and lumbering ferries churned the Pacific. Yachts glided and seagulls soared against the cloudless blue skies. A majestic white ocean liner slipped gracefully through the heads. Alex put his arms around Hannah's slender waist and pressed his lips to the silky halo of her hair.

'If we were on that liner,' he murmured softly, 'where would you want it to be going?'

Hannah sighed dreamily. 'Europe... America... the Greek Isles... Asia... the Arctic...'

Alex chuckled and held her closer still. 'But if you had to choose just one?'

'It would definitely be Europe. Except I've always had a secret desire to visit Disneyland.'

'Some day I'll show you the world,' he murmured against the soft curve of her cheek. He turned her to face him, and she saw the promise in his eyes and the burning passion of his love. 'What time is our first appointment?' he asked huskily against the trembling softness of her lips.

'Not until one o'clock,' she whispered, and slipped her arms around his neck.

'That gives us plenty of time!' He picked her up and carried her into the bedroom to lay her gently down on the huge four-poster bed. They undressed each other slowly, deliciously, tickling and teasing, stroking and kissing, tormenting, until neither could stand it any longer and their bodies joined together in a burst of heady passion that sky-rocketed them into orbit and tossed them around the planets. Afterwards they completely soaked the bathroom when they playfully washed each other under a cold shower. Wrapped in thick white towels, they snuggled together on the love-seat and took their time deciding what to order for lunch from the very impressive menu. After much deliberation they finally decided on dishes neither had ever tried before, and, when the exotic array was delivered to their suite, fed each other until all the tasty titbits were cleared from their plates.

At one o'clock they kept their first appointment at a branch of Hannah's legal firm, and Alex signed the last of the documents which proclaimed him the new owner of Paradise. They celebrated with cups of cappuccino at a little pavement café before Alex visited his engineers to talk about his plane's design.

'That's business for the day,' Hannah announced as they stepped once again on to the crowded Castlereagh Street.

'Not quite,' Alex corrected her mysteriously. 'We still have one more appointment.' He took her arm and guided her further down the street to a towering skyscraper. A lift zapped them up to the nineteenth floor to a firm of architects, where the smiling, attractive receptionist was obviously waiting for them. She greeted Alex by name and said Bob Carr was ready for them.

Once inside the modern and very spacious office Alex introduced Hannah to the young architect and asked if the scale model was ready.

'Right over here.' Bob Carr led them over to a display table and on top lay what Hannah first thought was a beautiful little village. She looked questioningly up at Alex. His eyes smiled down at her.

'Well, what do you think?' he drawled softly. 'Does it match your dream?'

Mystified, she looked again at the model. And then she understood. The little white cottages all had brightly coloured roofs, each a different colour. There was a schoolhouse, an infirmary and a recreation hall. Clumps of trees and shrubs surrounded miniature fishponds and on a little lake were several rowboats. Picnic tables and benches were scattered throughout the complex and there was a tennis court, a playing field and a bowling-green. It was more, so much more than she had ever dreamed. Overcome by emotion, she could only look up at Alex, her eyes swimming as she tried to put into words what was happening in her heart. But when he put his arm round her shoulders and drew her close to his side she knew no words were necessary. Discussions followed, but Hannah couldn't think of a single item to improve on the plan. Alex had thought of everything and so much more. When he led her back to the lift her face was flushed with excitement. Before the startled onlookers also waiting for the lift she reached up on tiptoe, pulled Alex's head down and gave him a long, hard kiss.

'You devil, you!' she exclaimed. 'You beautiful, wonderful, adorable devil!' And to prove she really meant it, she kissed that devil again!

When they returned to the hotel and Alex opened the door to their suite, they were confronted with the intoxicating scent of roses. Mystified, Hannah stepped into the room. Roses were everywhere—huge bouquets of them. On the writing desk, on top of the wardrobes, night tables, scattered across the love-seats, beside the french doors, outside on the balcony and even in the bathroom.

'Now I wonder how these got here?' Alex drawled innocently, but Hannah already knew. She was holding a card in her hand, signed by Alex, telling her he loved her. It was a wonderfully romantic gesture, and she was deeply touched. She went over to him, unbuttoned his shirt and laid her hands on the tanned, broad, muscular wall of his chest, her fingertips tingling at the feel of the silky black hairs as they skipped over them. She slipped the shirt off his powerful shoulders and proceeded to his belt buckle. She fully intended to thank her love for his gift of roses!

That evening they dined in elegant splendour at the hotel's famous revolving restaurant. The lights of Sydney twinkled below and danced across the harbour. Alex looked divinely handsome in black trousers and a white dinner-jacket which enhanced his dark colouring. Hannah had never looked more radiant. Her green velvet evening gown showed off the creamy smoothness of her skin and highlighted the greenish tints in the mysterious golden aura of her beautiful eyes. They held hands across the table, hers pale and delicate, his tanned and broad. His thumbs caressed the damp moisture of her palms and the candlelight which flickered between them highlighted the wondrous glow of their love.

'Will you dance with me, Miss Baker?' Alex asked in a husky drawl.

'I'd love to,' Hannah returned with an answering smile.

He held her in his arms and they swayed in tune to the soft, romantic music. He danced superbly and she barely felt her feet touching the floor. His arms tightened around her and his lips burned against her cheek. She slipped her slender arms around his neck and lovingly touched the coarse black hair against the smoothness of his collar. The intoxicating male scent of him filled her nostrils and the music entered her being. She wanted this night to continue forever.

'Excuse me, sir.' The discreet voice of the *maître d'hôtel* exploded between them. 'There's an urgent telephone call for you, sir.'

The colour drained from Hannah's cheeks. She looked fearfully up at Alex. His expression was grim, wary, his blue eyes narrowed. She clutched at his arm.

'It's Bartholomew!' she whispered hoarsely. 'Something's happened to Bartholomew!'

Alex gripped her firmly by the arm and led her back to their table before following the *maître d'* to the awaiting phone. He returned within minutes, and when she saw the expression on his face her insides shrivelled.

'What is it?' Her voice was barely above a whisper as she half rose from the chair. '*Tell* me!'

'It was Mimi.' He put a steadying arm round her quivering shoulders. 'Bartholomew's gravely ill. We must leave immediately. I'll tell you the rest in the plane.'

The following hour remained a blur in Hannah's memory. There was a vague recollection of swiftly packing their bags, of Alex settling their hotel bill, of a taxi speeding them towards the airport, of the plane taking off. But one thing she would always remember was the grim, bleak expression on Alex's face as he repeated what Mimi had told him.

'Bartholomew became ill shortly after I left the homestead,' he began in a tense voice. 'Mimi decided it was nothing more than flu and treated him accordingly. Then late this afternoon his temperature soared. She did everything possible but couldn't get it down, so she rang for the doctor. He couldn't come immediately. When he did, Bartholomew was delirious.'

Hannah swallowed hard. 'Is he... is he in hospital?'

Alex shook his head. 'There's a raging storm on the Coast. It would be too dangerous to move him in his weakened condition.'

Hannah felt encased in ice. Her earlier forebodings had proved correct. She didn't know how, but Bartholomew had sensed that she would be with Alex. As they approached the Coast's skyline lightning flashed about the plane and great buffets of wind knocked viciously at the structure. Torrents of rain splashed against the windscreen, and visibility was down to zero.

We're being punished, Hannah thought almost calmly. We put ourselves ahead of a troubled little boy and God is punishing us. Alex can't possibly land this plane safely, not under these conditions. We're going to die. Death will be our punishment for daring to love each other!

CHAPTER TEN

WITH all the skill of a trained fighter pilot Alex brought the shuddering, skittering plane down safely on to the slippery runway. The wind and the rain took their breath away as they raced towards the Mercedes. Hannah's evening gown and Alex's dinner-jacket were soaked through to their skins, but neither seemed to notice. Alex gripped the steering-wheel, his knuckles white.

Mimi met them at the door, her face grey with worry and fatigue. 'There's been no change,' she told them grimly. 'The doctor's still with him.'

The doctor looked up when Hannah and Alex entered the bleak starkness of Bartholomew's bedroom. He said a few quiet words to Alex, then left them alone. Bartholomew thrashed wildly in his bed, the lamp on the night table revealing the purple flush of a soaring temperature. His eyes were open, wild and staring, glazed with fever.

'Oh, Bartholomew!' Hannah cried, and sat beside him and touched his cheek. She was shocked by the heat. Her eyes were filled with anguish as she gently stroked back the wet hair clinging to his brow. Alex sat beside her, a cold compress in his hands to lay on Bartholomew's head. His eyes were heavy with grief and alarm.

Bartholomew's eyes stared unblinkingly into Hannah's tear-streaked face. '*Mom*!' he whispered hoarsely, and his hands groped frantically for her hand. Hannah held tightly on to them. 'Oh, Mom, I shouldn't have said it! I love you! I've never, ever hated you!' He struggled violently to sit up, his wild, torture-filled eyes pleading with Hannah to believe him. 'I shouldn't have said I hated you, because I don't! I don't! So please don't go away. *Please* don't leave us! *I didn't mean it*!'

Hannah and Alex listened in shock to the boy's tragic confession. 'It's all right, Bartholomew,' Alex crooned softly, his hand gentle and reassuring on the small tortured brow. 'We believe you.'

Bartholomew's head swung towards Alex. '*Dad*!' he gasped. 'You're *here*!' He grabbed Alex's hand and kissed it, over and over again. 'I thought you'd gone and taken Mom.' Suddenly he stopped kissing Alex's hand and instead grabbed his arm. 'Where are you going?' He started to pant. 'No, Dad! *No*! I didn't mean it. I love you—I don't hate you. I was just . . . just angry! Please don't go.' And then a final desperate plea, '*Please forgive me*!'

Bartholomew fell back against his pillows, his exhausted trembling body gradually relaxing until he drifted into a restless slumber. Hannah and Alex remained by his side, their eyes filled with pity and love. There was a muffled sound at the door, and they turned and saw Josephine and Annabelle clinging to each other, tears streaming down their pale little faces. Hannah and Alex immediately went to them. Alex put his arms around their shoulders and ushered them gently out of the room. They went downstairs to the kitchen. Hannah made steaming mugs of hot chocolate while Alex spoke quietly to the girls, their small hands held in the huge protective enclosure of their uncle's.

'You know your brother's been deeply troubled for some time now,' he said gently. 'We haven't been able to discover his problem, but now that we have we can begin to help him.'

'How?' Annabelle asked in a quivering voice.

'I'm going to ring your auntie Hilda and see if she can come and spend a few days with us. She was with your parents before the accident, and so was Bartholomew. Perhaps she can shed some light on what happened.'

The girls drank their hot chocolate, then Hannah took them to their rooms and tucked them into their beds. Their faces were sad and withdrawn as they bade her goodnight. Alex was still on the telephone with Auntie Hilda, so Hannah went into Bartholomew's bedroom. The doctor had gone. Bartholomew's fever had broken. Hannah gazed down at the troubled child. Even in sleep he appeared tormented. She sighed heavily and pulled up a chair to sit beside him. His hand moved and she gently touched it with her finger. His fingers curled around hers and he sighed in his sleep. When Alex came into the room half an hour later, the weary lines in his brow cleared and a tender smile softened the grim expression on his face. Hannah's body had slumped halfway on to the bed and she and Bartholomew were sound asleep, his hand still tucked in hers. Alex carefully removed it, lifted Hannah in his arms and carried her down the hall to a bedroom. She half awoke when she felt her evening gown being removed and then the blissful warmth of blankets covering her shivering body.

The following morning was grey and windy. Rain splashed against the windows. Alex knocked softly on her door and entered carrying a breakfast tray. He had changed into a warm beige sweater and chocolate-brown trousers, and his hair was still damp from his shower. He looked exhausted, and Hannah knew he hadn't had any sleep. Several times she had awakened throughout the long, dark night and had heard him tending to Bartholomew. He poured them both coffee and sat beside her on the bed.

'How is he?' Hannah asked quietly.

'Quiet . . . weak from the fever.'

'Does he remember anything of what he told us?'

'Vaguely. I think he thought he was dreaming.' He sighed heavily and put his cup back on the tray. 'Hilda will be arriving shortly. She's deeply concerned, of course.'

'Was she able to shed any light on the whole situation?'

Alex ran a hand roughly through his hair. 'Apparently Bartholomew had been quarrelling with his parents ... and his parents with each other.' His face darkened. 'There'd been talk of a divorce, and each threatened to leave the other. I was away in Europe at the time and had no idea what was happening. Anyway, according to Hilda, there'd been some trouble over Bartholomew's performance at school. His grades had slipped drastically. A family holiday had been planned, which was to double as a reconciliation, but because of Bartholomew's grades it was decided at the last minute to leave all three children at home with Hilda looking after them. Naturally they were disappointed, Bartholomew especially.'

'And so he said he hated them,' Hannah finished with a sigh.

Alex nodded, stood up and shoved his hands into his pockets. He looked out of the window, at the grey skies and driving rain. 'He also told them he wished they were dead!' He turned to face Hannah. 'That's what's been driving him, torturing him.' He shook his dark head. 'According to Hilda he told them he hoped they'd have a plane crash and both be killed.'

'And that's why he believes he killed them,' Hannah said sadly. 'What a dreadful burden he's had to bear.'

'Our job will be to convince him that many children say things they don't mean and never want to happen. It's all part of growing up and learning to handle our emotions.'

Hannah rose and joined him at the window. She took his hand and turned him to face her. 'We can do it,' she said softly, and reached up to smooth away the tired lines in his face. 'We've got to give Bartholomew back his life!'

Hilda arrived, and Hannah liked her immediately. She was fun-loving and gay and extremely childlike. The girls treated her like a not-very-bright older sister. They were all sitting in the study when Alex came in followed by Bartholomew. Hilda gasped at the sight of her pale young nephew. His face was drawn and he looked so thin. He was wearing pyjamas and a dressing-gown. He didn't greet his aunt, nor did he look at anyone else in the room. Instead he walked slowly over to the family portrait.

'I hate that thing!' he said softly.

Auntie Hilda gasped. 'Bartholomew! How could you say such a wicked thing? It's *beautiful*!'

'No, it's not. It's ugly. It's...it's not *us*!'

Hannah understood. The picture represented the bad times and was a constant reminder of when things were wrong. She went over to Bartholomew and put her hand on his shoulder. He immediately stiffened, but at least he didn't brush her hand away. Alex joined them. He too placed a reassuring hand on the young shoulder. 'What should we do with the painting, Bartholomew?' he enquired gently.

Josephine came up with the solution. 'The grandparents have plenty of pictures of us, so let's give it to Auntie Hilda.'

'Yes, let's,' Annabelle agreed promptly. Alex met Hannah's eyes and they silently agreed. Alex removed the picture from the wall and handed it to Bartholomew. He walked slowly over to his aunt and placed it in her hands.

'Take good care of it,' he said gruffly.

Hannah made a leisurely tour of the grand old homestead. She remembered how it had looked when she had first come here, how bare and cold. Not any more, she thought as she fluffed up the colourful cushions on the sofas in the family room. Pictures hung on the walls and books cluttered the shelves. Scatter rugs brightened the wooden floors and everywhere there was the sign of children living in harmony.

Slowly she made her way upstairs. She felt nostalgic. Perhaps it was a sign that the baby was on its way. She laid her hands on her swollen tummy and smiled. She and Alex had been married for eighteen months now, and at times the road had been rough and sometimes painful. But it had gradually smoothed, and she was proud of their successes.

Josephine's confidence had grown, she had put on some much-needed weight, sported a becoming new hairstyle and was captain of her class. Skin-care products lined Annabelle's bureau instead of make-up, and the gaudy theatrical clothes and jewellery lay in a box, forgotten in her closet. Bartholomew no longer blamed himself for his parents' deaths, but every so often Hannah saw dark shadows in his eyes and would wonder sadly if they might always lurk there. She paused now in front of his bedroom, and smiled. Although he was too young to shave she could smell the musky scent of aftershave and knew he splashed it on each morning before he left for school. It was rumoured that he had a girlfriend. Posters lined his walls, baseball and cricket bats stood in a corner and other male paraphernalia was scattered about his room. He had definitely moved in!

Hannah continued her tour to her and Alex's bedroom. She stood at the window and gazed out at the direction of Paradise. The cottages had been built and the complex was complete. Several retired teachers came each day to coach the youngsters up to State standard. A 'big brother' and 'big sister' scheme had been set up, and, because the older children were made responsible for the younger ones, drug and alcohol abuse had been quickly eliminated. There was always a band of crafts people showing up to teach the youngsters various skills. At any one time there was never less than a hundred young people living, working and studying there. Hannah sighed deeply. It had been a truly worthwhile dream.

And there had been other successes. Alex's plane had hit the world by storm, and he was in heavy production now keeping up with the demand. His markets had extended to Europe and North America. Mike Thompson had certainly been correct when he said everything Alex Drummond touched turned to gold! Even now he was working on yet another brilliant design. Hannah sometimes worried that her man might be working too hard, but she knew he thrived on it.

As she gazed dreamily out of the window, Alex appeared over the crest of the hill. Her heart swelled and hammered with the love she felt for him. He saw her at the window and his handsome face broke into a broad smile. He lifted his hand to wave, and when she was about to do the same, she felt the first pain.

Alex rushed her to hospital, and six hours later Hugo Alexander entered the world. The following day, Alex proudly escorted the three children to view the new arrival. As Hannah waited for them she became increasingly aware of a nervous tension in the pit of her stomach. The children were still so vulnerable. What if they didn't accept this precious bundle as their brother but merely looked on him as a cousin? The family would once again be divided, and it was time for them to finally close ranks.

Alex ushered the children in. Their eyes zeroed down at the sleeping infant. They were not impressed!

'Where's his hair?' Annabelle growled. 'I don't like bald babies.'

'Is he supposed to be so small?' Josephine enquired anxiously.

'He doesn't look like a Drummond,' Bartholomew observed gravely.

The baby's blue-black eyes suddenly flew open and he seemed to glare at the critical trio before opening his mouth wide and howling in protest. The startled children stepped back in alarm and stared in astonishment at this small bundle of fury. Baby Drummond stopped his howling, smacked his lips contentedly and settled once more into a peaceful slumber.

'I suppose he's got enough hair,' Annabelle decided.

'His hands are big,' Josephine added.

'And so is his mouth!' Bartholomew grinned. 'He seems tough enough. Tough enough to be a Drummond.'

Hannah felt weak with relief. Their tiny son had passed the test. Alex chuckled and gently lifted his son to place him in Hannah's outstretched arms. The children crowded around her, their fingers gently stroking the baby's tender skin.

'Is he our brother?' Annabelle asked.

Hannah held her breath.

'Of course he's our brother!' Bartholomew declared with a fierce pride in his voice.

A photographer wandered down the hospital corridor. His job was to take photos of newborn infants and their mothers. He stopped at the door of Hannah's room and smiled at all the fuss being made over this particular infant. Alex looked up and saw him there, and motioned with his hand. No one but he heard the soft click of the camera before the photographer moved on.

When Hannah and Alex arrived home with the new baby, Mimi was the only one to greet them at the door. Hannah tried to swallow her disappointment that the children weren't there. 'Go into the den,' Mimi ordered. 'I've made tea and sandwiches.'

'Perhaps I should put the baby to bed,' Hannah said to Alex. 'You go ahead and have your tea and I'll join you later.'

But Alex insisted she have her tea now. He took the child from her arms and opened the door to the den. The children sprang up to greet her. 'Surprise! Surprise!' they shouted gleefully. And then, 'Look round you, Hannah. Tell us what you *see*!'

She saw the picture. It was hanging over the mantel. It was the most beautiful portrait she had ever seen. She was holding the baby, Alex's arms around her, the children all over her, their hands touching, their eyes glowing, their faces tender in love. She looked from the painting to her family surrounding her now. Their expressions were the same, and her heart soared. Annabelle and Josephine rushed into her arms and hugged her tightly. When they had released her, Bartholomew stepped forward. 'Welcome home, Hannah,' he said gruffly, and she heard the catch in his voice.

Hannah smiled. 'I was just about to say the same to you. Welcome home, Bartholomew.' She held out her hands and he took them, then he flung himself into her arms and hugged her fiercely. Over his head, Hannah's tear-filled eyes met Alex's and she saw in his face what she was feeling in her heart. They were home now, all of them, safe at last. The shadows had finally disappeared.

Six months later the entire Drummond family excitedly tossed streamers over the rail of the white luxury liner which would cruise them to America and to Disneyland. An elderly couple seated on deckchairs watched the happy family. The wife turned to her husband and said:

'It's easy to see that young family have never known a care nor a worry in their entire lives.'

Her husband agreed. 'Easy to see all right!'

Accept 4 FREE Romances and 2 FREE gifts

FROM READER SERVICE

Here's an irresistible invitation from Mills & Boon. Please accept our offer of 4 FREE Romances, a CUDDLY TEDDY and a special MYSTERY GIFT! Then, if you choose, go on to enjoy 6 captivating Romances every month for just £1.80 each, postage and packing FREE. Plus our FREE Newsletter with author news, competitions and much more.

Send the coupon below to: Mills & Boon Reader Service, FREEPOST, PO Box 236, Croydon, Surrey CR9 9EL.

Next Month's Romances

Each month you can choose from a wide variety of romance with Mills & Boon. Below are the new titles to look out for next month, why not ask either Mills & Boon Reader Service or your Newsagent to reserve you a copy of the titles you want to buy – just tick the titles you would like and either post to Reader Service or take it to any Newsagent and ask them to order your books.

Please save me the following titles:	Please tick	√
THE SEDUCTION OF KEIRA	Emma Darcy	
THREAT FROM THE PAST	Diana Hamilton	
DREAMING	Charlotte Lamb	
MIRRORS OF THE SEA	Sally Wentworth	
LAWFUL POSSESSION	Catherine George	
DESIGNED TO ANNOY	Elizabeth Oldfield	
A WOMAN ACCUSED	Sandra Marton	
A LOVE LIKE THAT	Natalie Fox	
LOVE'S DARK SHADOW	Grace Green	
THE WILLING CAPTIVE	Lee Stafford	
MAN OF THE MOUNTAINS	Kay Gregory	
LOVERS' MOON	Valerie Parv	
CRUEL ANGEL	Sharon Kendrick	
LITTLE WHITE LIES	Marjorie Lewty	
PROMISE ME LOVE	Jennifer Taylor	
LOVE'S FANTASY	Barbara McMahon	

If you would like to order these books in addition to your regular subscription from Mills & Boon Reader Service please send £1.80 per title to: Mills & Boon Reader Service, Freepost, P.O. Box 236, Croydon, Surrey, CR9 9EL, quote your Subscriber No:................................. (If applicable) and complete the name and address details below. Alternatively, these books are available from many local Newsagents including W.H.Smith, J.Menzies, Martins and other paperback stockists from 9th July 1993.

Name:...

Address:...

....Post Code:..........................

To Retailer: If you would like to stock M&B books please contact your regular book/magazine wholesaler for details.

You may be mailed with offers from other reputable companies as a result of this application.
If you would rather not take advantage of these opportunities please tick box ☐